ARRESTED BY LOVE

A LONG VALLEY WESTERN ROMANCE NOVEL – BOOK 3

ERIN WRIGHT

WRIGHT'S ROMANCE READS

To Jasmine the Writing Cat:
Thanks for all the snuggles. This book literally wouldn't
have been the same without you…

CHAPTER 1

WYATT

NOVEMBER, 2016

WYATT MILLER WANDERED down the snack aisle of the Mr. Petrol's at 11:30 at night. Nothing like trying to find dinner in the aisles of a convenience store. Did onion rings and beef jerky count as a balanced diet? He could consider the onion rings to be his vegetables, and the beef jerky to be his protein.

He grimaced. Some days, living in a small town really sucked, like when grocery stores prided themselves on being "open late" – all the way until nine at night.

He pulled Lay's Salt & Vinegar off the display.

Look, more vegetables.

He wasn't sure a dietician would approve, but then again, there was almost nothing in this convenience store that a dietician would approve of. He really should just drive to Franklin and go grocery shopping there, but that was 30 minutes away and he just didn't feel like it. When he died, his headstone was going to read, "Too lazy to drive to Franklin; died of a heart attack from eating junk food from Mr. Petrol's."

Just then, a vehicle pulled up outside. Well, "pulled up" made it sound like the driver was in control of their actions, but as Wyatt watched, his bag of chips forgotten in his hands, he saw the Jeep stop *just* in time to keep from crashing through the front windows of the convenience store.

Oh shit.

He knew that Jeep. There was only one orange camo Jeep in the valley.

The driver's side door swung open and out swaggered Richard. Wyatt couldn't tell if Richard was swaggering because he was so arrogant and full of himself – always a possibility – or because he was drunk – definitely another possibility.

Wyatt reminded himself to breathe in, and then out. And then repeat it all over again. He couldn't react the way he wanted to – a punch to the face – so he needed to just stay calm. That's what everyone would tell him, anyway.

He knew that. It was a matter of remembering that. And doing that.

No matter how good a punch to Richard's face would feel.

Richard stumbled into the store and from two aisles over, Wyatt could smell the fumes rolling off him.

Drunk it was.

Richard managed to make his way over to the beer case without taking out an end-cap display, nothing short of a miracle really, and snagged a 24-pack of Budweiser.

A 24-pack? Really? When you're already this wasted?

Wyatt was having a hard time breathing again and he realized that he'd smashed the bag of chips in his hands into a tiny ball, chips spilling onto the floor from the busted seams of the bag. Richard didn't seem to notice the noise, though, swinging the 24-pack up onto the counter and swiping his debit card moments later.

Breathe in, breathe out.

Wyatt was hoping that at any moment, the cashier would stop him. Surely, he'd realize that giving Richard more beer at this point was a truly awful idea.

Right?

Richard took his beer and began stumbling towards the door.

The cashier wasn't going to stop him. Wyatt could feel the rage begin to boil up inside of him.

"Why did you sell him that beer?!" The words burst out of Wyatt like gunfire. He couldn't stop himself from asking any more than he could stop himself from breathing.

"Dude, do you know who that is?" the cashier responded with a shrug.

"Of *course* I know who that is," Wyatt ground out.

"Well, my probation is almost up. Just a month more and I'm out of the system. I'm not pissing off the judge's son."

That was it. Wyatt threw the mangled bag of chips to the floor and sprinted for the door. He wasn't about to stand by and let Richard take someone's life because he happened to share genetic material with the only judge in town. Oh *hell* no.

He burst out the front door of Mr. Petrol's. Richard had finally managed to get his key into the ignition and turn it. Wyatt grabbed the door handle and yanked it open.

"Whaddya want, killer?" Richard slurred, blearily focusing his eyes on Wyatt.

"Hello, brother. Nice to see you again." Wyatt pulled back his fist and planted it squarely in the middle of Dick's nose.

CHAPTER 2

ABBY

"GOOD MORNING, DADDY," Abby said in a sing-song voice as she walked into the sheriff's office.

So, she may or may not have known *exactly* what he was going to say in response before he even opened his mouth. She'd opened with the "Daddy" greeting because the mood in the office told her that he was in a particularly foul mood, and, well, sometimes it was a little fun to screw with her father's head.

"You know the rules," he scolded her. "When either one of us is in uniform, we have to be Sheriff and Deputy. I get enough raised eyebrows for hiring my own daughter. Don't make that worse, especially today of all days."

"Oh yeah? What's going on?" She sat down in front of his gigantic desk, intrigued. Usually, her dad didn't let stuff get to him, but the way he was pacing back and forth in front of the only window in the room, she was starting to think something bigger than dispatch showing up late, as always, was going on.

"You might as well hear it from me because it's about to become your problem," the *sheriff* said.

"Hold on. You're the guy in charge. Aren't problems your department?"

"Actually, my job is deciding who problems belong to and making assignments according-ly," he retorted.

She stifled the urge to roll her eyes. Some days, being the daughter of the sheriff could be more than a little annoying.

"So, what's causing such stress in the squad room?"

"You'll never believe who's in the back."

"You're right, I have no clue. I actually

turned my radio off last night and since no one called, I assumed everything was fine."

"Wyatt Miller," he said.

"Wow," Abby said, just as shocked as he'd thought she'd be. She stared at him for a moment, trying to process what he'd just said. She suddenly felt awful for being bratty when she first came in. As his daughter, she needed to be more supportive, a little less sarcastic. "Are you okay?"

"You'll never believe *why* he's in here," he said, ignoring her question.

"Did he tear up O'Malley's over a game of pool again?"

"No, he beat up Richard Schmidt in the parking lot of Mr. Petrol's."

"He what?!" she exploded. "How in the hell could he do something like that?!"

Dad just stared at her and that's when Abby got past the shock of Wyatt beating Richard up − although really, that was going to take a while, if she was being honest with herself − to how hard it must be on her dad to be dealing with this. This was like a maelstrom of every shitty possible circumstance, thrown together.

"Oh my God, Dad, are you okay?" She jumped out of her chair and went to give him a hug.

"Abby…" He held up his hands defensively, warding off her hug, something that stung her more than she would've guessed it would. She changed directions and headed for the open office door instead.

"Don't give me that," she said, shutting the door and turning back to him with a sympathetic look. "There are times that you're still my father, no matter how many badges you stack between us, and this is one of those times."

"Okay, fine." He took a deep breath and looked her in the eye. "To be honest, I'm not doing that well. That's why I want you to be the one who handles this. I kept it together for the most part when I talked with his brothers. However, I could feel my restraint slipping," he said, rubbing his forehead. "This *seems* very cut and dry. I should want him to get what's fair, but given everything that's happened, I can't stop feeling like he should get more than what's strictly speaking 'fair.' That's the problem. If I can't control my personal feelings and I screw this up, he won't even get what he rightly deserves."

"So…you want *me* to take this on?" At his nod, she asked him, a bit sarcastically, "What makes you think I can control my temper better than you can?"

"You're a better person than I am," he said simply.

"That's not true and you know it."

"Well, everyone will have to deal with him at some point, but I'm trying to remove myself from the situation as much as possible. I don't want my personal feelings to get in the way. I'm hoping that because you have some distance and you're the shift commander, you'll be more effective than I would be in making sure nothing goes wrong."

"Are you okay?" She knew she sounded like a broken record but she couldn't help worrying as she studied her father. His blood pressure could get too high and—

"Yeah, I'm great," he said, trying and failing to act happy and normal, and then he slammed his fist down on the desk. "No, I'm pissed as hell right now. I cannot *believe* that it was *that* asshole who beat up the judge's son. That's Wyatt Miller for you – he thinks he can solve all the world's problems with his fists, and he never stops to think about whether or not he should be involved, and especially whether or not his fists should be involved. Next, he'll be down at the bar, telling yet another round of people that he knows how to run their farms better than they do. I've never met such an arrogant, know-it-all piece of shit in all my life."

He stopped and stared at Abby, breathing heavily.

"I'm pretty sure it's clear that I shouldn't be involved with the day-to-day business of keeping Wyatt here," he said, and Abby thought she could hear just the barest hint of sarcasm in his voice when he said that.

She just bit her lip and nodded. Even though Wyatt's comment to the whole town about how her dad didn't know how to run a farm and he could show him how to do it had happened what felt like eons ago, it was obvious her dad still hadn't gotten over it. She wasn't sure if he ever would. At least her dad realized that he needed to keep that space between them.

"All right, Sheriff, what do you need me to do?"

"Just do your job as shift commander and jail supervisor. Treat him like any other detainee, but if you have any problems, just take care of it. And for hell's sakes, don't give his lawyer any wiggle room. You have my full authority to just act as you see fit, as long as you leave me out of it."

"So can I ask the obvious question?"

"Which is…?"

"Why not just declare this to be a conflict of interest and ship him over to Ada County?"

"The last thing that I need is that jackass proving that I can't run my own jail."

"Right," Abby said. She really didn't have

anything else to add to the conversation, a new one for her.

"What I need you to do, and I do realize that I'm laying a lot on you, is keep this all together and keep me out of trouble at the same time. Just take this on and act as you feel is appropriate. I'll back you in whatever you do."

She nodded.

"From afar," he added.

She left him sitting there and headed for her problem in the back.

CHAPTER 3

WYATT

*G*OOD HELL, *I FEEL HORRIBLE.*

He was sick and felt like he'd lost a fight with a grizzly bear, and to top it all off, he was dreaming about his brother Stetson yelling at him to wake up. If there was one way to ruin a day from the start, it was to deal with his sniveling little brother in his dreams. The snotty little bastard couldn't even leave him alone when he was trying to sleep.

Finally, his brain made the connection that Stetson wasn't in his dream, but actually was yelling for him to wake up.

His eyes finally opened and dear God, it

was bright. His head roared in protest. What the hell had he done to himself?

He didn't recognize the room. He could hear Declan and Stetson arguing about something and he didn't care what it was about. All he cared about was getting them to shut up.

"This isn't the time for your petty bull, so knock it off," he heard Declan saying.

"Whatever, Mom," Wyatt managed to say but it didn't sound quite right when it came out. "Where the hell am I?"

"You're in jail," Declan said, in that patronizing voice he used when he was trying to calm his older brother down.

Wyatt hated that voice so damn much, but he let his brother get away with it for some reason he couldn't recall at the moment. It'd come to him later.

He swung his legs over the edge of the bed he was lying on and tried to stand up. The whole world shifted to the right and Wyatt decided to sit back down instead. Just for a minute.

"Why the hell am I in jail?" he finally got out.

"You decided to be a one-man vigilante justice squad and beat the hell out of Richard Schmidt," Stetson said, glaring at him, arms crossed across his chest.

Oh.

Right.

He remembered that now.

He was pretty sure that admitting this to a counselor or a judge would just prolong the time spent behind bars, but on the other hand, smashing his fist into *Dick's* nose was the best Wyatt had felt in a long time.

"He was drunk. I tried to talk him out of driving and he would have none of it." Wyatt shrugged, which sent more pain surging through him. The world had gone red with that first punch, and looking back on it, he wasn't quite sure what'd happened. It was all just a haze of anger and retribution. Maybe "tried to talk him out of driving" wasn't exactly true, unless one considered "punching with fists" to be talking, in which case he did a *lot* of talking.

Asshole called me Killer. *He deserved every punch he got, and then some. If there was ever a shitty trick to pull, that was it.*

"Listen, I know after what happened, you two aren't exactly bosom buddies," Stetson said sarcastically. "But that doesn't mean that you get to punch him when you get a hankering for it. Perhaps a phone call to the police would've done the trick."

"Why? So he could get thrown in jail for the night and then walk away scot-free, like he always does?"

Declan pushed himself between the two of them. "Wyatt, we've talked about it and we think that maybe just having you hang out here for a day or two might be useful."

Wyatt swung his gaze back towards Declan. Out of all of the people in the world he thought would be on his side, Declan topped that list. Declan *was* that list.

He never thought Declan would betray him like this.

At the look on Wyatt's face, Declan put his hands up defensively. "Wyatt, you put him in the hospital. He has three broken ribs and they're probably going to have to do plastic surgery on his face to put the bones back where they're supposed to go. I know you think that you were justified, but you can't just let loose and whale on people like that."

"No one died and made you the king of the world," Stetson said flatly. "You have to figure out that you can't punch your way through life."

"Yeah, whatever. Leave me the hell alone," Wyatt said. "You two just want me to fail and are using this as a chance to make that happen. God, even my own family is turning against me. Without me, you two would be nothing. *I* am the one who thinks about all the stupid shit you don't even know about. Go ahead, leave me in here. You'll be back in a day, begging me to save your sorry asses."

He turned his back on them and waited for them to leave.

"I'll watch your farm. Jorge is taking care of most of the work, so I'll just make sure he gets the help he needs," Declan offered. "You can get the help you need in here."

"Yeah, don't do me any favors," Wyatt said sarcastically and then changed his mind. "Actually, do me one favor. Keep Stetson off my place. I don't need to clean up his messes when I get out of here."

Neither of them said a word. He waited for Stetson to have something smart to say, but he stayed silent. Finally, Wyatt couldn't handle it anymore.

"Just leave. You two are pissing me off."

He listened to the clicking of their cowboy boots on the concrete floor fade away and for the heavy clunk of a door shutting before he lay back on the cot and closed his eyes.

Why do people always pull this shit on me?

CHAPTER 4

ABBY

*A*BBY WALKED DOWN the jail block to Wyatt's cell. It was his big day, and she was the lucky officer who got to take him down to the courtroom. He'd spent the last week split between snarling at her every time she walked by, and reading western novels. She figured that this hearing was going to go as well as could be expected, which was to say horrifically awful.

She wasn't about to tell Wyatt this (or her father, for that matter), but she felt bad for Wyatt. Her dad would have a heart attack if he heard her say this, but since that first morning in his office, she'd discovered that her father's recounting of why Wyatt had landed in jail was...missing a few pieces. A few *important* pieces. Wyatt hadn't just blindly punched Richard for the hell of it 'cause the sky was blue and the wind was blowing in from the west.

Okay, sure, Richard didn't deserve to end up in the hospital but she was beginning to see that when it came to Wyatt Miller, her dad wasn't acting rational either.

"Ready?" she asked, stopping at his cell door and holding up her keys and handcuffs. He grunted at her, swung his legs over the side of his cot, and tossed the Louis L'Amour paperback into the corner of his bunk. He slid his hands through the opening in the door so she could cuff him, and then after she unlocked the door, he began silently walking towards the front, as she followed along behind him.

With such a winning personality, it's hard to see why everyone just doesn't love and adore him. She tried not to roll her eyes as they went. If Wyatt had half the likability that his looks had, he would have a lot more fans in the world.

It was a short docket today – just Wyatt's case and a couple of speeding tickets. Of course, Judge Schmidt put Wyatt last because if given even a small chance to be an ass to Wyatt, he was going to take it.

Finally, it was Wyatt's turn.

"The State of Idaho Vs Wyatt Miller," the court reporter called out. Wyatt shuffled forward, his lawyer by his side. Abby leaned against the wall of the courtroom, holding her breath. This could go okay, or it could be a trainwreck. Considering that it was Judge Schmidt and Wyatt, though, she was pretty sure that a betting man would count on the latter.

"So you're here on charges of assault and battery, huh?" the judge said, leaning down and staring at Wyatt over the top of his spectacles. "I always knew this day would come. Of course, I never thought that you'd lose it on my son—"

"Judge Schmidt, we'd like to ask for a change of venue," Wyatt's lawyer interrupted. Interrupting the judge was almost never a good idea, but then again, this whole situation was just a circus and a half. There were no rules any longer. She wouldn't be surprised to see the judge pole-vault over his bench and land some punches of his own. "I think it's clear that there's a conflict of interest here. We would like to get the venue moved to Ada County."

The judge sat back in his chair, smirking. "Fine by me. But I hear their dockets are pretty full this time of year, what with the holidays and all. You'll probably be waiting a while for your hearing."

"Which is why we'd like to ask for bail for Mr. Miller," the lawyer smoothly interjected. "It's late fall and thus a farmer like Mr. Miller is still wrapping up his harv—"

"But with such a high-flight risk," the judge said with a twist of his lips, "I can't let him out. Who knows where he'd go if let out of jail until his hearing in Boise."

"Your honor," the lawyer said pleadingly, "Mr. Miller has only ever lived in Long Valley. He owns a farm here. His family is here. He's the very definition—"

"—of a high-flight risk," the judge said, cutting him off. "I know *Mr. Miller's* background quite well and don't need to be reminded of it. If he wants to move his hearing to Ada County, so be it. But I won't have him escaping justice under my watch. This case is hereby moved to Ada County; Mr. Miller is to be kept in the Valley County Jail until his case can be heard in Boise. Dismissed." He rapped his gavel on the wood in front of him.

Abby stared at the judge for a moment, horrified. She'd worried that the judge would take advantage of being able to preside over Wyatt's hearing, but even she hadn't expected him to pull *this*.

If Wyatt couldn't finish harvesting his sugar beets, then they'd rot in the fields and he wouldn't be able to make his yearly payment to the bank. His brother Stetson hadn't made his payment to the bank the previous fall, which, through a lucky twist of fate, was how he'd met his wife Jennifer, but somehow, Abby didn't think that Wyatt would be half as lucky. This could ruin Wyatt financially, and the judge knew it. His dryland wheat had already been harvested, but he made most of his money from his beets, and the judge was well aware of that fact.

Damn asshole piece of shit, screwing around with Wyatt like this. He knows exactly *what he's doing. The only way Wyatt escapes this mess is if his brothers step in and help him, and they have their own farms to run. Plus, I heard them that morning they stopped by the jail after Wyatt was arrested; I don't know if they're going to be inclined to do his farming for him. This judge is using his power to mess with his former son-in-law and there's not a damn thing I can do about—*

She heard someone clear their throat right behind her, and then a touch on her elbow. She whirled around, finally breaking her stare from the retreating judge, to find Wyatt's lawyer standing next to her. "I think my client is in need of your services," the lawyer said softly.

Right. She was supposed to walk him back to his jail cell. She shot a bland smile at the lawyer before putting the handcuffs back on Wyatt, trying – and most likely failing – to hide her inner turmoil. As she snapped the cuffs around his wrists, she couldn't help noticing his muscular arms, tanned from a summer under the sun, and how his hair curled around his nape, just a little too long for convention but perfect for running her fingers through.

She cleared her throat as she shook her head, making herself focus on her job.

It was going to be a long few weeks.

CHAPTER 5

WYATT

*H*E SAT IN HIS JAIL CELL, waiting impatiently for the counselor to show up. That wasn't something he ever thought he'd be doing – waiting for a counseling appointment wasn't exactly something he did all the time, let alone finding himself looking forward to it – but here in jail, he was beginning to look forward to *any* changes to be had in his suddenly monotonous life.

The truth was, he was bored out of his skull. This was the longest he'd ever gone without working since he'd turned eight and had started regularly helping his dad out in the fields. Even during the winter, he was able to go for rides on the horses or work on tractors out in the barn.

So day in, day out of nothing but reading Louis L'Amour, eating food from Betty's Diner, and walking out in the courtyard for 30 minutes at a time was, quite simply, slowly driving him insane.

Well, that and watching Abby walk past on her rounds. And walking to his cell with his dinner tray. And then spending time bantering with her over whether or not tomatoes were really edible (which of course, he was right and she was wrong and tomatoes just weren't edible, no matter how much people protested otherwise).

But other than Abby and all Abby-related activities, jail was sheer boredom. He lay back on his bunk and stacked his hands underneath his head, staring up at the water-stained ceiling. Talking to a counselor…he hadn't done that since high school, and that was a career counselor, not a help-you-with-your-emotional-shit counselor.

This counselor was 100% his lawyer's idea, arguing that telling the judge in Boise that he'd been trying to get help while awaiting his hearing could only help his case. Wyatt didn't think the judge would give a rat's ass – his former father-in-law here in Long Valley sure as shit didn't – but…

He was bored.

Bored out of his ever-lovin' mind.

Bored enough that talking to a counselor sounded like a fine idea.

Which had to be the very definition of boredom.

He was glad Shelly wasn't there to see him in jail, rotting away. She'd be so disappointed in him. Of course, him punching her brother probably wouldn't have helped matters any, either.

On the other hand, if she was still around, he wouldn't have had any reason to punch her brother.

He heard the door open at the end of the cell block, thankfully interrupting that internal never-ending cycle of guilt. Abby's voice floated down towards him as she walked beside who he guessed was the long-awaited counselor. "He's back here – we have conference rooms you can meet in if you'd like."

Just hearing Abby's voice was…nice. Wyatt swung his legs over the side of the bed and watched as she walked towards him, hips swaying as she did so. He'd always appreciated a little meat on a woman's bones – whoever thought that sleeping with a bag of bones was sexy was just this side of completely insane – and Abby managed to have curves in *all* the right places.

Not that he was looking at the sheriff's daughter in *that* way.

Of course.

"Yes, that would be appreciated." The counselor's voice, cultured but friendly, finally had him turning towards his new distraction from insanity. She was a little older, maybe late 50s, with short brown hair peppered with gray, and square-rimmed glasses that gave her a bookish appearance. He'd never met a counselor in real life, and he wasn't sure what he'd been expecting, but now seeing her...

She looked just like what he imagined a counselor would look like. If he'd ever bothered to imagine a counselor, which he hadn't, of course.

He stood up from the bed and moved towards the cell door. He put his hands through the door's opening so he could be handcuffed, when the counselor put her hand up to stop Abby. "I prefer that my clients not be handcuffed while talking to me. It makes it hard to relax if you're in metal bracelets. I believe that I can trust Mr. Miller to be a perfect gentleman while we talk?" She looked straight at him, her gray eyes assessing him as she spoke.

He nodded without breaking eye contact. "I give you my word," he said solemnly. Not that he'd ever attack a woman, but considering his history of beating people up who didn't agree with his viewpoint of the world, he understood her desire for assurances.

"Good enough for me."

Abby shrugged and hooked her cuffs back on her belt. "Then I'll just lead you two to the conference room," she said, unlocking and swinging the cell door open for him. He brushed past her and unconsciously inhaled as he passed. Lemons. How was it that she always smelled like lemons? It was the damndest thing, in the most awfully perfect way. It was his favorite scent – clean and pure without being cloying – and if he didn't know any better, he'd think that Abby picked it on purpose to drive him crazy.

Which obviously she hadn't, considering that she didn't know it was his favorite scent.

Which made the whole thing even more maddening.

She walked behind them as they made their way to the front and to the right. After they got settled at the conference table, she pulled the door shut behind them, telling the counselor, "Just come get the officer on duty when you're done," and then disappeared behind the wooden door.

Wyatt felt a sense of loss at her disappearance that he didn't want to begin to explain to himself. Or anyone else for that matter.

The counselor smiled at him, a friendly yet professional smile that told him that she would be a confidant, but not a friend. He respected that.

"Mr. Miller, may I call you Wyatt?"

"Yes, ma'am, that'd be fine."

"You may call me Rhonda."

He nodded once. "Rhonda."

"Wyatt, I understand that you have some history with the man you beat up, a Richard Schmidt. Is that true? Or did you simply get a hankering for a good ol' time, and begin swinging at him because you hadn't punched someone lately?"

He couldn't help the small smile that grew around the edges of his lips. "I'm sure it depends on who you asked," he said blandly. "I'm sure there are people in this town who'd believe that's exactly why I was punching Dick."

"Dick? I thought he preferred to go by Richard." She arched a perfectly manicured eyebrow at him. He grinned boyishly at her.

"Oh, he does. Which is *exactly* why I call him Dick. It's just a lot more appropriate for his personality."

She cracked a smile of her own at that. "Well, why don't you tell me about your relationship with Richard. We can start there."

Wyatt settled back in his chair. "How long do we have?" he asked sarcastically.

"As long as we need," she responded without missing a beat. "Normally, I schedule my clients in one-hour increments but I don't have anyone else in Long Valley to see today, so I can spend the afternoon chatting with you if that's what you'd like."

She was purposefully pushing back at him; she knew he wouldn't want to spend all afternoon talking to a counselor any more than he'd want to spend all afternoon taking ballroom dancing lessons.

She had a spine. He liked that.

"I married Dick's sister, Shelly, seven years ago. I got along with Dick and his father, Mr. Schmidt, fine in the beginning but it quickly became apparent that they didn't think I was good enough for her. Which I probably wasn't, but truth be told, what husband is good enough for their wife?"

"So your father-in-law is Judge Schmidt?" she asked.

"Ex-father-in-law," he corrected.

"You got a divorce?"

"No." He heaved a sigh, and shifted in his seat uncomfortably. This was the hard part. This was the awful part. It was the one good thing about living here in Long Valley – everyone knew his story. He didn't have to tell it over and over again. He didn't have to face these facts that made up his shattered life. "She died. Car wreck. One year ago. My daughter was in the car with her. They both died at the scene."

She just stared at him assessingly, nodding once to indicate she'd heard him, so he continued. "My father-in-law and brother-in-law blamed me for it."

"Were you driving?" she asked.

"No. I was at home."

"Then why did they blame you?"

"Because I'd asked her to go get the milk that night. I'd just gotten home – it had been a long day – and Shelly told me we were out of milk. Normally I'd go and get the milk because you don't want to buckle in a five year old to drive to Franklin just to buy milk but I was tired and didn't want to make the drive. I was being selfish." He stared at the far wall, a non-descript print of a seashore hanging there, and felt his throat tighten with frustration and tears.

No, not tears. He didn't cry.

Just frustration.

"What time was it?" the counselor asked softly.

"Time? Evening. Maybe around nine or so."

The counselor let the silence fill the small room, expanding, pushing down on him, but he didn't say anything and so she finally, blessedly, continued. "So when you saw your brother-in-law—"

"*Ex*-brother-in-law."

"Your ex-brother-in-law at the convenience

store, you decided that it was time to discuss this…with your fists?"

He nodded. It may not be politically correct to admit it, but yeah, that was exactly how it went down.

"Did he do anything to provoke this…discussion?"

"Yes!" He stopped, realizing that his voice was overwhelmingly loud for the tiny room they were in. He breathed in, trying to reign in the feelings washing over him, but the injustice of it all had been gnawing at him for weeks now. It was time for *someone* other than his lawyer to hear his side of things, dammit.

"He was driving drunk. He almost took out the front side of Mr. Petrol's. He was there to buy more beer, and the cashier let him. Told me that he wasn't about to piss off the judge's son, not when his probation was almost up. Dick was already in his ugly-ass orange camo Jeep when I came outside to stop him from driving away. Things got out of hand pretty quickly."

"Why didn't you call the cops instead?"

"That's what everyone says I should've done, but I say bullshit. The cops would've come, arrested him, and he would've been out by morning. His dad would've made sure that he got off scot-free from it. That would've been the end. Dick Schmidt would've gotten away with it. Again. I couldn't stand the thought. This whole valley…it's like that everywhere, for everyone. Special treatment if you know the right people, can pull the right strings."

"Have you thought about moving away from here?"

"Away?" he echoed dumbly. "And go where? My farm is here."

"I'm pretty sure that there are farms elsewhere," she said with a quirk of her lips.

"But my family is here. I've never lived anywhere else. I couldn't leave Long Valley." He felt panic welling up inside of him at the idea, and he was surprised by the strength of it. He'd spent most of his life hating Long Valley, hating the good ol' boys club that was so prevalent in the area, but when faced with the idea of leaving it, he was terrified. This was his home.

His great-great-grandparents helped settle the area. He couldn't leave it.

"Okay, so if you don't want to sell and move elsewhere, what can you do to make your time here in Long Valley more pleasant? If you won't change your circumstances, how will you change your outlook on those circumstances?"

That stopped him in his tracks. "Change his outlook"? That too had never occurred to him.

He was beginning to realize that there were many things that hadn't occurred to him, and he wasn't particularly sure he appreciated that insight.

CHAPTER 6

ABBY

CHLOE STIRRED HER COFFEE and looked at Abby over the rim of it as she took a sip. "So, what's been happening in your world? Anything exciting?"

"I wouldn't call it exciting," Abby said with a grumpy sigh, "but Wyatt Miller has been happening."

"Oh, I heard about that! Is it true that he beat up Richard Schmidt in the parking lot of Mr. Petrol's?"

"Yes." Abby knew she wasn't strictly supposed to gossip about the jail inmates, but she couldn't help herself. She had to talk to *someone* about it, and the other choice was her dad, and that *so* wasn't happening. Chloe was her closest friend, and thus by default, was immune from the rules about what she was and wasn't allowed to be told. The best friend version of "spousal privilege."

"Soooo…how has he been as an inmate?" Chloe asked inquisitively. "He's never been the most outgoing of guys the few times that he's come into the restaurant." Chloe worked as a waitress at Betty's Diner, the breakfast and lunch diner across the street from the courthouse. She'd worked there since she moved to Sawyer eight years earlier.

"Oh man, I'm sure he was downright joyful when he came to the restaurant compared to now. He's…not the most cheerful of men."

Which really was too bad. All of the Miller boys were handsome, but there was something…something undefinable about Wyatt that made her heart go into overdrive every time she was around him.

Which she'd admit out loud about the same time that she set her hair on fire.

She looked down and fiddled with her napkin. Was there no way to control her damn hormones? She was a grown adult, not a love-struck teenager. She knew that Wyatt was a good idea, just like shooting herself in the foot was a good idea.

Now she just needed to tell the butterflies in her stomach that.

"Oh my God, you like him." Chloe stared at her, wide-eyed with shock. "You like Wyatt Miller!" she hissed, leaning across the wobbly table.

"I do not!" Abby hissed back in true seventh-grader fashion, but she couldn't help herself. It would not exactly be a bonus to her career if this rumor were to get out. Sawyer was a small town, and it didn't take much to start a rumor. Usually nothing more than a glance that lasted two seconds too long and people were suddenly getting married.

Or at least the gossip made it sound like that.

"Okay, so Ms. I Don't Like Wyatt Miller, what color are his eyes?"

"Dark blue," she ground out. Obviously. Who wouldn't notice his eyes? It wasn't like she had to pay special attention to him in order to notice his eyes. They were bright and captivating and she'd have to be blind not to notice that they reminded her of stormy clouds hanging over the mountains, promising rain and thunder and lightning.

It didn't mean anything at all to notice that.

"Interesting. And what *doesn't* he like to eat?"

"Well," Abby said defensively, not really wanting to answer but not sure how to get out of it, "he has an almost vitriolic hatred of tomatoes. Not ketchup or salsa, just raw tomatoes. I've been meaning to tell you that I think you should leave them off his sandwiches when you make them at the restaurant. He's pretty good about eating the sandwiches, other than the tomatoes of course, and he eats most kinds of chips, but he's not real fond of the Sun Chips—"

"Listen to yourself!" Chloe practically

howled with pleasure. "I told you, I told you, I told you!"

Abby sat back, her face turning a brilliant red under Chloe's watchful gaze. "He's…a little on the handsome side," she finally allowed, "but nothing more than that. My father would have a heart attack if I dated Wyatt Miller. Lordy, can you imagine?"

"I'd pay money to see your dad be told that. I think they'd need a spatula to scrape him off the ceiling." Chloe grinned at her and Abby rolled her eyes. Chloe liked needling people just a little bit, which was *exactly* why they were best friends. But even Abby couldn't imagine telling her father that she was dating Wyatt.

"The whole fistfight in the parking lot… Well, Wyatt was trying to stop Richard from driving drunk, and after what happened to his wife and child, can you really fault him for it?"

"That's true," Chloe mused, "but you have to admit that Wyatt tends to solve problems with his fists rather than his head. This isn't the first time he's beaten someone up." She shot Abby a pointed look and Abby grimaced.

"Yeah, I know. Dammit, I wish his personality matched his looks. He's a damn good-looking guy. He's so handsome, and yet, so negative."

She thought back to the last few days. That wasn't *strictly* true.

Ever since his visit with the counselor, he'd been a little different. She wasn't going to say *cheerful* because she wasn't sure if Wyatt was capable of cheerfulness, but not quite so sullen and pissed off. He said please and thank you. He said hello when she walked by. When he'd run out of Louis L'Amour books in the county jail library, she'd stopped by the Friends of the Library building in town and bought a grocery sack full of paperback westerns for him, telling herself that she wasn't treating him any differently than she'd treat another inmate.

Normally, they just didn't house long-term inmates, so they didn't have the problem of running out of reading material for them. She'd go buy westerns for any inmate that they had longer than a week or two.

Any inmate at all.

"I wish you could see the look on your face right now," Chloe said with a huge grin. "I'm not sure if you're trying to fool yourself or not, but you sure aren't fooling me. Wyatt is damn easy on the eyes, and I'm pretty sure you've noticed that. You can't tell me otherwise."

Abby shrugged. "Doesn't matter one way or the other. After New Year's, he's going up to Ada County to be heard by a judge there. Hopefully they'll look at the extenuating circumstances, and the fact that Wyatt's been locked up for weeks and weeks previous to his hearing in Boise, and they'll let him go home. It's too late for him to finish his harvest; either his brothers stepped up to the plate and did it for him, or he's screwed financially. But either way, he'll be out of my hair soon enough."

"I'm gonna wash that man right out of my hair," Chloe sang softly, grinning teasingly, "and send him on his way."

"Exactly."

And she ignored the pang that shot through her at the thought. That was indigestion, and nothing more.

CHAPTER 7

WYATT

"MILLER, the phone is for you." Officer Morland worked his way down the cell block towards Wyatt's cell. Wyatt froze, numbly setting down the worn paperback western Abby had brought him, and just stared at the cop. He hadn't seen his brothers since the morning five weeks ago when he'd told them to go away.

But who else could it be? It wasn't like friends would be calling the jail just to chat and catch up on old times.

Maybe his lawyer?

Morland opened up the cell door, letting

Wyatt past him before following him up to the phone banks. "You have 10 minutes," he said, not unkindly, before heading back up front.

With a steadying breath, Wyatt picked up the phone. "He–hello?" he said, hating the waver in his voice.

"Hey Wy, it's Declan."

Oh. *Good.*

If Wyatt had to pick a person in the world to call him, it would've been Declan. It was kind of shocking how nice it was to hear his brother's voice, actually. Wyatt closed his eyes against the unwelcome prickle in his eyes. When in the hell had he become such a softy?

Being locked up sure was messing with his mind. He had to get out of here before he turned into a blubbering fool.

"Hey. How are things?" he got out, a little more gruffly than he'd intended.

"Pretty good! Working together with Stetson and Jorge, we got your sugar beets harvested and shipped off, so that's taken care of for the year. A real good harvest, actually. Your bookkeeper will go over the payments with you, but you should be able to easily make your yearly payment to the bank with the way prices have been looking lately."

"Thank you," Wyatt broke in. He wasn't used to thanking people, but his harvest was something that had been weighing on his mind. He'd thought about inquiring after it through his lawyer, but his pride hadn't allowed him. To find out that his brothers had come through for him in the end…well, even he could manage to rustle up a "thank you" for the occasion.

"Sure, sure. Listen, Christmas is coming up soon – I thought I should stop by and see how you're doing. Chat a little."

"Oh yeah?" Wyatt said, taken off guard by the offer. He hadn't had a single visitor since they'd locked him up, unless he counted his lawyer or his counselor. Which Wyatt most definitely did not. "That'd be good. I'll be here, so just…stop by whenever you want." *As if I have a choice*. The unspoken truth hung in the air.

"Great, I'll be by this afternoon."

"Okay, uhh…I'll see you then." It felt weird to be making plans to hang out with his younger brother, but a good weird. A break from Larry McMurtry, the western author he'd moved on to after finishing every Louis L'Amour he could lay his hands on, sounded damn fine right about then.

Declan hung up, but Wyatt held the phone against his cheek a little longer, unwilling to lose that connection just yet. Along with the welcome news of the harvest and his impending visit, Declan also mentioned the unmentionable: Christmas.

Wyatt was going to be spending Christmas in jail, after already missing Thanksgiving, which had to be just about the most depressing thought he'd ever contemplated.

Which is why he *hadn't* contemplated it until now. In fact, he'd done a damn good job of ignoring that fact up to this point, quite on purpose, thankyouverymuch.

But as always, Declan was thoughtful enough to realize that he'd be alone on Christmas, and wanted to spend some time with him beforehand. Christmas was only four days away, and no doubt, Declan would be spending Christmas Day at the Miller farm with Stetson and his new wife, Jennifer. That was where the Miller brothers always gathered to celebrate the holidays.

Except for this year.

"You done?" Morland asked, popping his head through the door and peering at Wyatt.

"Yeah, I'm done," Wyatt said, hanging the phone back in its cradle.

He followed the guard back to his cell, the door swinging back into place with a squeak. Wyatt climbed back onto his bunk bed and stacked his hands behind his head, staring up at the water-stained ceiling again. It'd been nice to hear his brother's voice, and it was nice to think about seeing him that afternoon. He was surprised to realize that the anger and hurt he'd felt when Declan and Stetson had left him that day in his cell, not bailing him out like he'd wanted, wasn't nearly as sharp or painful as it'd been before.

Was he forgiving his brother? He rather thought he was, and was surprised by the fact.

He'd have to tell Rhonda when she came on Wednesday.

Of course, then she'd just ask what was going on with the sheriff, and had he forgiven him yet? Wyatt felt his chest tighten at the thought. There was one son-of-a-bitch he was never going to forgive. The man hadn't bothered asking him for the truth all those years ago; had just listened to the rumors swirling around town and had judged him guilty. If the sheriff was going to be the judge, jury, and executioner without even bothering to listen to the defendant, then why should Wyatt forgive him?

It had happened so long ago – his wife and daughter were still alive. His dad was, too. Wyatt had been so damn frustrated with his dad and Stetson at that point. Years of arguing with them on how best to run a farm, and the two of them didn't listen to a word he had to say. Finally, he'd had an opportunity to buy his own place and get out from underneath the thumb of his father, and he'd jumped on it like a dying man on a glass of water.

It wasn't his fault that it was the sheriff's

farm that he was buying. It wasn't his fault that the sheriff had had a couple of bad water years and hadn't been able to make his payments to the bank. It wasn't his fault that the sheriff had had his farm repo'd and put up on the auction block.

He'd caused none of those problems and yet, the sheriff still blamed him because Wyatt had the temerity to buy the man's livelihood out from underneath him.

All of that probably wouldn't have made him and the sheriff besties, but then, Wyatt had to go and celebrate at O'Malley's the night of the signing with a couple of his buddies. He was so excited; he was finally going to show his father and brother how a *real* farm was run.

Damn pronouns. Wyatt knew which "he" he'd meant when he'd said, "I'm finally going to show him how a farm is run," but by the time the rumor got back to the sheriff, that "he" had become Sheriff Connelly. The way the people of Sawyer saw it, it was bad enough that Wyatt had bought a farm that had been foreclosed on, but to brag about it afterward was just downright awful.

He'd tried to explain. He'd tried to tell a few people that the "he" was his father, but actually, it was really his brother. It was Stetson who'd insisted on raising cows on the Miller farm. Everyone knew that the Millers were farmers, not cowboys. They raised wheat and beets, not cows, dammit.

But that was Stetson to a T, going and screwing everything up by raising those damn cows of his. Wyatt had tried to tell them that cows got sick and they shit everywhere and they up and died on you for no damn reason at all, and only the village idiot would want to mess with them, but then again, didn't that almost perfectly sum up Stetson?

In the end, Stetson kept his cows and his dad died and Wyatt bought the sheriff's farm off the auction block and everyone in the county believed that Wyatt believed that he was a better farmer than the sheriff. After years of this persistent rumor floating around, Wyatt had long ago quit trying to explain himself and just accepted that the sheriff was never going to invite him over for tea and cookies.

But now…now he was stuck in the sheriff's jail until at least January 3rd, his court date in Ada County, and he had to see Abby Connelly every day and he had to pretend that he saw nothing in her that he wanted, because the sheriff would okay him dating his only child right about the time that he burned the courthouse down to the ground. Wyatt had a better chance at becoming president of the United States than he did of winning over the sheriff.

Well, no matter what the counselor said on the topic, Wyatt could forgive Declan and move on, but he was never going to forgive the sheriff. He asked for it, refusing to even listen to Wyatt's side of the story.

There were some lines that you just didn't cross, and the way Wyatt figured it, that was one of 'em.

CHAPTER 8

ABBY

ECLAN CAME THROUGH the front door of the sheriff's office, removing his hat as he entered the room. "Ma'am, how are you?" he asked, coming up to the front counter.

She rolled her eyes and grinned. "Declan, we graduated a year apart from each other. I'm pretty sure we can move past the 'ma'am' part."

"That's true. I s'pose my momma would only toss and turn in her grave instead of plain ol' rolling over if I were to call you Abby."

"I won't tell her if you don't." Abby grinned at the middle Miller son, and as they walked to the back to the jail block, she wondered anew why she didn't find Declan attractive. Well, she did, but in a totally clinical way. He was handsome and tall and kind and thoughtful and damn good-looking…

And he didn't do a thing for her. Not a damn thing. She couldn't begin to imagine kissing him. It would be like kissing her brother, if she'd been blessed with such a creature. Maybe it was because she'd grown up with him…? She didn't know the cause of her complete and total apathy towards Declan, but she could state categorically that it was there.

Unlike his older brother, who despite his warming trends, still wasn't the most pleasant human being to be around. He could be prickly and grumpy and snarky…

And just being around him made it hard for her to breathe.

Which just proved that you can't choose who you're attracted to, because no one in their right mind was attracted to Wyatt Miller. Not unless they were hankering for pain and misery.

Which Abby was most definitely not.

"Hey brother!" Wyatt said, swinging his legs off the bunk and hurrying the few steps to the cell door. "How are you?" They shook hands through the bars as Abby worked to unlock the door. Once she got it unlocked, Declan stepped inside and Abby pulled the door closed behind him.

"Just holler when you're done," she said, and headed back up front, leaving the brothers with their privacy. They weren't large enough to have a visitor's area, so Declan would just have to hang out with Wyatt in the jail cell until he was done. She heard Wyatt's low chuckle as she shut the door behind her as the brothers began to chat, and she smiled to herself. It was good to hear him laugh. It wasn't a sound she'd heard in years, and even as rusty as it was, it was still nice.

She got some paperwork done and finally heard Declan calling out through the thick door separating the front office area from the cell block. She hurried into the back and saw the two brothers standing side-by-side in the cell, watching her walk towards them. Seeing them next to each other made her realize how similar they looked, despite the blond tints to Declan's hair compared to the dark, rich auburn locks that Wyatt was sporting. He hadn't had his hair cut since he was booked all those weeks ago, and his hair was starting to get longer than convention usually dictated.

She liked it.

She fumbled at her keys on her belt and finally got the jail cell unlocked. "Thanks," Declan said with a smile as he stepped out of the cell. She glanced over at Wyatt and found that he also had a small smile on his lips. He looked…almost friendly.

God, what a difference a visit from a family member makes.

She closed the door, making sure it locked firmly in place and then escorted Declan back up front to the main entry area to sign him out.

"Hey, I know it's a lot to ask," Declan said, his voice low, "but I need to talk to you about Wyatt's dog, Maggie. She's not dealing well with Wyatt being gone. She's quit eating and she won't move from the front porch. She just sits there, staring down the driveway, waiting for Wyatt to return. I think she may waste away to nothing if we don't get her in here to see Wyatt soon. He's already lost his wife and daughter; I just can't stand the thought of him losing his dog, too."

Abby took a deep breath, the heartbreaking story wrenching at her heart. Wyatt may have screwed up; Wyatt may have made poor life choices, but that didn't mean his dog should die.

She also knew her dad would freak out if he found out that she was letting Wyatt's dog in here.

But hadn't her father said to "just take care of Wyatt" and that he'd back her in *whatever* she chose to do?

He probably hadn't been thinking about dogs when he'd said that, but hell, that was just too damn bad. If he was going to offload Wyatt Miller onto her shoulders, he couldn't then complain about how she dealt with that problem.

She just had to hope that the dog didn't have fleas.

"Bring her on by. When were you thinking?"

"Tomorrow afternoon. Will you be here?"

The unspoken part of that question was that they both knew that if Declan brought a dog in while a different officer were on duty, they'd be turned away at the door. It had to be done while Abby was here, and they both knew it.

"Yeah, from 3 to 7. I'll be out on patrol before then."

"I'll be here between 3 and 7, then. Thanks." With a flash of a handsome smile that did absolutely nothing for Abby, Declan headed for the front doors.

She sank into the office chair behind the front desk with a sigh. She was about to do royal battle with her dad over this, and even though she knew she was right, that didn't mean it would be easy.

CHAPTER 9

WYATT

OOWWWW ooooweweweew ooooweweweww...
Wyatt heard Maggie Mae's distinctive howl just as he heard nails scrambling on the concrete floor and he jackknifed up, his heart pounding. Surely, surely, they weren't letting Maggie into the jail. That just wasn't something Sheriff Connelly would allow.

But Maggie came scrambling into view, her legs going every which way on the concrete as she tried to launch herself through the bars at Wyatt.

*Oooweweww ooooweweww ooooweweweww...*She howled with delight, shoving her head through the bars, her tail wagging so fast, her hind legs kept falling over. She was literally quivering with delight.

He launched himself at the bars, letting her tongue lap at his face, wrapping his arms around her through the bars, hating the cold steel in the way, loving the fact that his dog was here.

Here!

How did she get here?

Declan and Abby rounded the corner, a little out of breath as they caught up to Maggie Mae. Abby was pulling her keys off her belt and working them into the lock as Maggie continued to bathe his face with all of the love and happiness her heart contained. He couldn't help it – he laughed, letting the joy that was welling up in him spill out.

"You let my dog in here," he said around his laughter, wonder filling his voice, staring up at Abby. She finally got the cell door open and convinced Maggie that she could get to Wyatt a little easier if she went around to the open door, rather than continuing to try to force her way through the bars.

Although, as she launched herself at Wyatt, knocking him back onto the concrete floor, causing him to burst out laughing again, he suddenly realized that getting between the bars would be easier for her right now than it really should've been. Running his hands up and down her flanks, he could feel her ribs.

He looked up at Declan, who was grinning with happiness, but his eyes were dark with worry.

"Has she not been eating?" he asked around her tongue, which was busy cleaning up his face and then over to his ear.

"Not a damn thing. She's just been wasting away, refusing to eat or drink, and refusing to move off the front porch. I know she seems like a bundle of energy right now, but I think she's been saving that energy up for the last five weeks because she's hardly moved all that time. I started to worry that she'd die of heartbreak."

Wyatt felt that like a punch to his stomach. Maggie was totally blameless; had never done anything but love and sometimes obey and then love some more. She didn't deserve to go through that.

"Thank you," Wyatt said softly, looking back and forth between Abby and Declan. "This is the best Christmas present I ever could've asked for."

Declan reached over and pulled some items out of a bag that Wyatt hadn't even noticed he'd been carrying. He had been busy fending off Maggie, who was now on a self-appointed mission to clean his other ear, but still, he was usually more observant.

"I brought some food and water," Declan said, putting bowls on the ground and pouring Kibble into one and bottled water into the other. "I was hoping that with her here with you, she'd be willing to eat and drink. If she won't, I'll have to take her to Vet Whitaker and see what he can do. She may need to go onto an IV drip."

But at the sound of Kibble hitting the bottom of her food bowl, Maggie Mae launched herself off Wyatt and dove into her food bowl like she was starving.

Which, of course, she was.

As she alternated between eating and gulping down water, Wyatt pushed himself off the concrete floor. He didn't know how to thank Abby – shake her hand? Give her a hug? She was his jailer. He couldn't exactly send her a thank-you card.

But he had no doubt in his mind that Abby's father would've absolutely said no to this idea. This was all her doing – there was no question on that.

In the end, he looked at her and said simply, "Thank you. It means a lot. I...thank you."

And then stopped, because he didn't have any other words to say. She just dipped her head in acknowledgment and headed back up front, pulling the cell door closed behind her as she left. "I'll check on y'all in a minute," she said quietly, disappearing and giving them privacy.

"Thanks for her, Declan," Wyatt said, nodding towards his dog who'd finally started to slow down on her food consumption. He was a little worried about her getting a stomachache but the idea of taking her food away from her just didn't sit well with him. He'd let her decide when she was full.

"Merry Christmas. To both of you." Declan shrugged, downplaying what he did. "I know that being in here during Christmas won't be easy, and I thought that Maggie Mae was the best present anyone could give you."

That was Declan, all right. Always thinking of others.

Which, of course, made him think about what a difference there was between Declan and their youngest brother, Stetson. Stetson had his head so far up his own ass, Wyatt was surprised he could still walk straight. He sure seemed to have won the lottery when he convinced Jennifer to marry him. Wyatt gave them three years of her putting up with Stetson's bullshit before she gave him his walking papers.

Pushing those thoughts away, he asked Declan, "So, what are you guys going to be doing for Christmas this year?" There was a golf-ball sized lump in his throat that he had to talk around. He didn't used to be this emotional and he wasn't exactly sure he appreciated the change. "Is Carmelita making her world-famous roast beef and potatoes?" *And homemade cinnamon rolls? And gingerbread cookies?*

Stetson lucked out with *two* women in his life – Jennifer to love him and Carmelita to cook for him. When Wyatt had bought his own place, he'd wanted to hire his own Carmelita, but had never managed to find someone as amazing as her.

Some days, Wyatt could find ten reasons to hate Stetson before breakfast, and thirty before noon.

"I don't know what they're planning," Declan said with a shrug. "I'm going to be spending it here with you."

"What?!" For the second time that afternoon, Wyatt felt like he'd been punched in the gut, but this was a positive punch, if such a thing existed. "You can't miss Christmas at the farm!"

Even when Declan and Wyatt had moved

out and bought their own places, they'd always, always gone back home for Christmas. Stetson may have inherited the family farm without doing a damn thing to deserve it, but that didn't matter when it came to Christmas. The Miller Farm was home for all three of the brothers, and always would be, no matter who their father gave the farm to in his will.

Declan just shrugged. "Stetson and Jennifer have friends they can invite over if they want to. They're lovebirds; they won't even notice that I'm gone. You're all alone here. It didn't seem fair."

"How'd Stetson take this news?" Wyatt asked suspiciously. Declan may be *laissez faire* about this idea, but he was pretty sure Stetson wasn't.

Declan grinned wryly. "Let's just say that I'm probably off the Christmas card list for a while."

Wyatt grinned back for just a moment but quickly felt the smile die away. Here was yet someone else who was innocent, who was being hurt by his actions.

"So you'll be coming back tomorrow?" Today was Christmas Eve Eve, if such a thing existed. Wyatt had only kept tabs on the day of the month so he could keep a countdown going of his hearing in Ada County, where hopefully, he'd be heard by a judge who gave a damn about justice.

Maggie flopped to the floor, finally satiated for the moment, and began to snore.

Wyatt was happier already, having her nearby. It was amazing to him how much he'd missed her snores, something he never would've guessed before being shoved in here against his will.

"Yeah, I'll be back tomorrow. Let me talk to Abby for a minute, though." Declan turned and shook the cell bars, trying to make enough noise to catch the attention of Wyatt's beautiful jailer.

Now where did that come from? If there was any person in the world off-limits for Wyatt, it was Abby Connelly. She was his jailer, for starters. He'd bought her father's land from them off the auction block, and the town and her father hated—

He stopped that train of thought right there. His counselor had been trying to get him to let go of the negativity he'd been holding on to for so long, and that included not dwelling on choices made by others.

I can't control the thoughts or actions of others; I can only control myself.

Abby came heading back down the hallway, her hips swaying with a natural grace that caused Wyatt's thoughts to go a little further south than he'd intended, but he forced his eyes to focus on hers. He wouldn't let himself think about anything else.

He wouldn't.

She slid the key into the lock with a bright smile. "Y'all done in here?" she asked, looking back and forth between them.

"Listen, I need to chat with you for a moment," Declan said with a charming smile he normally reserved for Carmelita, as he tried to wheedle his way into another slice of her amazing peanut butter and chocolate pie. Wyatt wanted to tell him that Abby never brought pie back from Betty's Diner but rather only boring turkey sandwiches. Maybe that'd get Declan to stop smiling so much at her. There was no reason to smile that much at the jailer.

Beautiful jailer.

No, jailer.

End of story.

They pulled the jail cell door closed behind them and headed back down the hallway, towards the front. Wyatt dropped to his knees, running his fingers through Maggie's fur. She instantly sat up, panting, her tongue lolling out of the side of her mouth as she grinned at him.

Wyatt smiled back, but he felt grief well up inside of him as he felt the changes in her even clearer now that the initial rush of surprise was over. Her fur was thinner and more coarse to the touch, and her ribs…he could count every one of them, and the knobs of her backbone, too. She'd never been husky, but this…she was nothing but fur and bones.

"Oh girl, I'm so sorry," he whispered,

mumbling into her fur, stroking her endlessly as he spoke. She laid her head on his shoulder and sighed contentedly, finally where she wanted to be. "I really screwed this one up. Yeah, maybe Dick deserved to get a busted up nose for driving drunk and then being dumbass enough to go buy yet more alcohol, especially because of how his sister died, but that doesn't give me license to teach him using my fists. You'd be proud of me if you could hear me with the counselor. She's really starting to help. You, though, you don't deserve any of this. I'm so sorry…"

He heard his brother's footsteps echoing, making his way back down the hallway towards him, and he hurriedly straightened up and flashed a forced grin at Declan as he came to stand right outside the cell door. He looked at Declan and then past him, down the cell block, wondering where Abby was. "Ready to head home?" he asked hesitantly. How was Declan supposed to take Maggie with him if Abby wasn't there to unlock the door?

"Yeah. I'll be back tomorrow around noon.

I'll see if I can get Betty's Diner to make us some turkey and potatoes and I'll bring that with me when I come. A regular Christmas feast."

Wyatt couldn't stand it anymore. "Where's Abby? She has to unlock the door if you're going to take Maggie home."

"You're going to keep her," Abby said, her voice ringing out with warmth and joy at being able to give him the news. She came around the corner and flashed him a blinding grin. "At least until after Christmas. Maggie needs to gain weight, and she won't if separated from you. Plus, it's Christmas. I can't take your dog from you at Christmas."

Wyatt's throat closed up so much with unshed tears, he was quite afraid he was going to unman himself. He could not, absolutely could not, cry in front of Abby. It would be bad enough to let a few leak out in front of his brother, but not in front of Abby.

Unable to speak, he finally just gave a jerky nod of acknowledgment, looking at her with all the gratitude in his soul. She gazed back, a small smile on her lips, and he dropped his eyes, unable to hold hers any longer. Unwilling to acknowledge the heat sizzling through his veins at the sight of her.

Not

Appropriate

"Well, I'm gonna head home," Declan said into the silence. "I'll be seeing you tomorrow. And you too, Maggie," he said with a smile at her, who thumped her tail upon hearing her name.

Abby escorted Declan out to the front, and Wyatt sat back down on the cold concrete floor, Maggie settling herself down onto his lap like some grotesquely oversized teacup poodle. Maggie always liked to pretend that she was a lap dog, something she was definitely too large to be. Comfortably anyway.

Didn't stop her from pretending.

Wyatt couldn't stop running his fingers through her fur, noticing all of the subtle changes, wondering why Abby had been so nice to agree to this. It certainly hadn't been because of his winning personality. If his mother had been able to see how he'd treated Abby these last few weeks, she would've rolled over in her grave. She raised him to be better than this.

Wyatt gently pushed Maggie off his lap so he could move, and crawled up onto his bunk, scooting over to the side so Maggie could curl up next to him. As she settled back into sleep interspersed with snores, he stacked his hands behind his head and stared up at the ceiling.

He had a lot of thinking to do.

CHAPTER 10

ABBY

CHRISTMAS EVE. Abby stared at the pile of paperwork she needed to fill out and let out a huge groan. The very last thing she wanted to do was fill out paperwork on Christmas Eve of all days.

"Abby, get in here!" she heard her father thunder.

Okay, make that the second-to-last thing she wanted to do on Christmas Eve. The *very* last thing she wanted to do was get her ass chewed by her father.

She worked her way over to his office and stood in the doorway. "Yes, Father?" she asked, her tone dripping with artificial sweetness. He glared at her. Obviously, her sense of humor was not going to be appreciated today, no matter what day of the year it was.

"Why on God's green earth is there a dog in my jail? I can smell the mangy mutt from here!"

She stepped inside his office and closed the door behind her. She wasn't about to get into a shouting match with him where any ol' stranger walking by could hear them. Much better to get into a shouting match where they at least had a little privacy.

"Dad, you told me that you wanted me to take care of Wyatt Miller without any input from you. 'You have my full authority to act as you see fit, as long as you leave me out of it,' I believe were your exact words."

"I never expected you to—"

"And his dog was dying. You may not have much use for the man, but surely you don't think his dog oughta die. She was starving to death – refused to eat or drink, just spent her days watching for Wyatt to return. She wouldn't have made it another two weeks for him to come home, not at the rate she was losing weight."

She didn't tell her dad, but she'd arranged for Vet Whitaker to stop by the jail late last night and check on her. Paid for the vet visit herself. He'd said that she didn't have much left to her and another week or so and she would've died from starvation. He'd put her on some vitamins to help her regain her bone density and put some shine back into her coat. He'd told Abby that she'd saved Maggie's life.

No, she wasn't about to back down, no matter what *Sheriff* Connelly thought.

"Well, just make sure she doesn't infest the place with fleas," her dad harrumphed. "Then I'd have to add the cost of an exterminator to Wyatt Miller's bill."

Abby tried not to roll her eyes, physically anyway. That was her dad's way of conceding defeat without admitting he was wrong. At least he was going to stop shouting, which she considered to be a win in her book.

"When will Rios be here?" her dad asked,

in an obvious bid to change the subject. "You going to be able to come home tonight to light the candle?" It was one of the few traditions that they still continued to practice every year — lighting a candle for her mom on Christmas Eve. She had to make it back to her dad's place for that tonight. Officer Rios better be on time for tonight's shift; she couldn't stomach the thought otherwise.

"Hopefully. That storm hitting us doesn't look like it's going to end any time soon, and I don't know how much it'll dump on us today. I'll do my best."

"Good. See you at home, then." He brusquely dismissed her from his office. She hid her grin as she headed for the door. Some days, she had to wonder if it'd cause her father physical pain to be affectionate towards her. She just wasn't sure he was capable of it.

Except as the hours passed, the storm outside just got worse. After a dash across the street to the diner to pick up the evening meal, she'd hardly been able to see a foot in front of her face. By the time she got back to the jail, she was shivering uncontrollably from the cold. The flakes were whirling around in front of her face, making it hard to keep her eyes open without having the flakes sting them. It was dark, much darker than it should've been, even in a valley with mountains to the west, even with it being the dead of winter. She felt like she'd somehow moved to Antarctica without realizing it.

When she got back inside, she set the to-go containers down on the counter, noticing a flashing red light on the phone. She listened to the message with a growing pit of dread in her stomach. Rios wouldn't be able to make it in after all. He lived down a long dirt road with several steep curves in it. Apparently, one had filled in with snow to the point of being impassable.

Oh God, Abby was stuck at the courthouse for the night. Not just any night – Christmas Eve. She felt tears pushing upwards and she willed them away. She would survive. It was just a date on the calendar. Her dad and her could light a candle on a different night and that didn't mean that they loved her mom any less.

She snagged the take-out containers and headed to the back, where she found Wyatt and Declan arguing over the rules of the Farming Game. Oh, the Farming Game. Abby wouldn't have been surprised to hear that couples got divorced over that game. It was addicting and fun and everyone who played it ended up being bit by the Must Win at All Costs bug. A bug Abby was not immune to, either.

"When you land on that square, you can't just hit every harvest between there and February!" Wyatt argued. "That isn't farming like a pro, that's hitting the jackpot!"

"Who's hungry?" Abby jumped in, holding the containers aloft. She'd heard the Miller brothers sometimes got into fistfights. She really didn't want to have to referee one in her own jail.

"Oh wow, is it that late?" Declan asked, shocked. "Dammit, I was going to go get us a Christmas dinner from across the street. Are they still open, Abby?"

"No, but I bought a dinner for you also, Declan. I figured it wasn't nice to have the county buy food for Wyatt and I and then not serve you anything. And they served up some real nice grub today. Turkey, mashed potatoes, gravy, and even a small slice of pie for every-one. Said it was Christmas, so why not?"

Wyatt caught her eye, the first time they'd made eye contact since she'd gone back there, and said simply, "Thank you." His eyes looked suspiciously moist, and she was sure he was pushing down emotions.

It wasn't easy to be away from family at Christmas, and for the first time since grumpy, prideful, rough-and-tough Wyatt ended up in her jail, Abby actually felt pity for him. She'd felt pity for his dog; she'd felt pity for his brother. But Wyatt…he'd gotten his ass into this mess.

Yeah, maybe Richard would've gotten away with driving drunk because his father was the county judge. But maybe not. Either way, Wyatt needed to learn how to solve problems without using his fists. That wasn't asking too much of a grown adult.

Except…

Maybe it was the season. Maybe it was seeing how sweet he was with his dog; that even now, she was lying next to him, her snout on his leg, watching the discussion with interest, or more likely hoping that some of that food in Abby's hands would somehow fall into her waiting mouth.

But whatever it was, when she smiled back at Wyatt, it was with a little more warmth than she'd intended. His dark blue eyes were warm and friendly and…sexy.

Forcing herself to abruptly end that train of thought, she began divvying out the food along with utensils and bottles of water. While she was serving up the food, Wyatt and Declan cleaned up the Farming Game, ribbing each other good-naturedly about who would've won if only they'd been able to play a full game. When Wyatt started saying, "As the older brother, I know how to farm better than you, so of course I would've won the game," Abby shoved his food into his hands, interrupting his little speech.

"Perhaps as a farmer, you're also amazing at eating?" she asked sweetly.

He glared at her for a moment and then solemnly said, "I am amazing at eating. There is no one better at eating than I am!" Everyone cracked up laughing, including Wyatt, his stony face breaking into a beautiful smile.

Abby heard Declan say something about how this explained why Wyatt was getting a spare tire around his waist, and Wyatt volleying back, heckling his younger brother as only brothers could, but Abby wasn't really listening to any of it. Her mind was caught on his smile. His gorgeous, high-wattage smile. Her breathing had stopped at the sight of it, but her heart had tripped into double-time.

She frantically thought back, trying to re-member if she'd ever seen Wyatt smile in their entire lives – a genuine, happy, huge smile. With only three years between them in school, he'd always been this older, cute guy who was way too serious.

But now, seeing him smile…

It changed his face, his personality. He lit up like a Roman candle.

He was beautiful.

"Abby. *Abby!*"

"Sorry, what?" she asked, turning back to the guys with a blank smile.

"You okay? You disappeared there for a minute."

"Oh yeah," she said, forcing her blank smile to grow more genuine. As genuine as a forced smile could become, of course. "Just worried about everyone out on the roads tonight. It's really bad out there. I don't know if it's a good idea for you to drive home, Declan."

"Is it that bad?" He put his fork down into his mashed potatoes, and then maneuvered his way out of Wyatt's jail cell, a space only meant to house two men but instead was housing two men, a woman, and a dog with a damn loud snore.

She'd left the cell door ajar – locking herself in with her prisoner didn't seem like a real great plan, and anyway, Wyatt wasn't going to go anywhere, she'd stake her life on that – so Declan slipped out and down the hallway to stick his head out into the jail yard.

Abby looked awkwardly at Wyatt, not sure what to say without the buffer of his brother to pave the way between them, until Maggie let out a snort and began running frantically on the floor. Except her body was sprawled out, her head on Wyatt's lap. She was in the grips of a very realistic dream, from the looks of it. Her face twitched as her body moved, her paws slicing through the air. Wyatt caught Abby's eye and they began laughing together at the absurdity of Maggie's movements.

"I think she's catching a rabbit. Hopefully, she'll be able to actually catch one in her dream, unlike when we're out on the farm," Wyatt said dryly.

"She can't catch rabbits out in the field?"

"Oh no, she's way too dumb for them. They outsmart her every day of the week. Sometimes, I think they sit back on their back haunches and stick their tongues out at her as she goes chasing after them. As soon as she gets close, down a rabbit hole they go, and poor Maggie. She has no concept of object permanence. Like an 18 month old, as soon as the rabbit is gone, she can't remember it ever even being there. One time, she went—"

"You weren't kidding, Abby." Declan's voice broke into their conversation and startled, she turned towards him. She'd forgotten he'd even left the cell. She'd forgotten he was even there. She'd been so engrossed in Wyatt's story, she'd forgotten about everything.

"Yeah?" she asked, trying to mask her surprise and worry at how easily her mind let her just forget about everything but Wyatt Miller for a moment.

He stepped into a bar of light and she could see him then – covered in a thick layer of snow, obscuring his light brown hair completely.

"How long were you out there?" she gasped, staring at him.

"You look like the Abominable Snowman," Wyatt put in.

Yup, these two were definitely brothers.

Declan ignored Wyatt, which was probably a good plan, and instead focused on answering Abby's question.

"Only a couple of minutes. I went for a little walk around the courtyard, propping the door open with my wallet so I wouldn't get locked out there. But damn, it's really coming down. I know the other deputy couldn't make it in, Abby – I wouldn't be surprised if there's a huge mess when this storm finally blows through. I've never seen anything like it before. It's a wall of white. I could barely see my hand when I stuck it out in front of me." He wiggled his hand in front of himself to demonstrate.

He came into the jail cell, clomping across it in his cowboy boots, until he could slide down into place against the far wall. His every step left a puddle of water behind.

Before Wyatt could raise a fuss about what Declan was doing to the floor of his cell, Abby scrambled to her feet.

"In the case of emergencies, I have a checklist of items to double-check. I'll be back in a minute. If we end up losing power, I will have wanted to make sure all of this was taken care of when I could see where I was going."

She headed out, pulling the cell door closed behind her this time, and headed for the front office. It was time to stop making googly eyes at the cute-if-total-pain-in-the-ass farmer in her jail cell and start doing her job.

CHAPTER 11

WYATT

"Do you remember that? I didn't think Mom would let me live to the ripe old age of 12 after that stunt." Wyatt grinned at Declan, happy for a moment at the memory. Those were truly the "good ol' days." It was before their mom had passed away. It was before their dad had decided to give the whole Miller legacy to the youngest sibling in the family, instead of to the oldest like he should have.

It was before a lot of the shit went down between him and Stetson.

"At least you could walk after Dad's paddling. I never thought I'd walk again after he found out I'd brought all of my frogs into Mrs. Westingsmith's room and let them go. I tried to tell him it wasn't on purpose but he paddled me anyway." Declan shrugged with a sorry-not-sorry grin on his face.

"I always meant to ask you – was it on purpose?" Wyatt asked, laughing.

"Oh hell yeah. There was a science test that afternoon and I'd spent the night before riding my horse and preparing for a 4-H event and so I was completely unprepared. I figured I could get paddled for having let a whole passel of frogs loose in my teacher's room, or I could get paddled for getting an F on a test. At least the frogs would be more fu—"

"Hey you guys, we may be in for it tonight," Abby said, walking up to the cell and cutting Declan off. "I just tried to start the backup generator to make sure it was ready to go in case the electricity went out, and it won't even pretend to turn over. I don't know what's going on, but if we don't ready for the electricity to go out right now, we could be in big trouble if it does."

She turned to Wyatt with an apologetic shrug. "I have to leave you in here, but Declan, I'd sure appreciate your help in rounding up supplies."

"Sure thing." Declan pushed himself off the floor and hurried to the cell door. She let him out and then locked it shut behind him.

"We'll be right back," she said to Wyatt, and with an unconsciously sexy sway of her hips, she and Declan hurried down the jail block to gather supplies.

With a quiet groan, Wyatt leaned his head back against the wall. What had he already told himself about sexy women named Abby Connelly? He couldn't get involved. He couldn't even look. It wasn't fair.

What else wasn't fair? Being stuck in his cell while Declan got to go *do* things. Wyatt wished he could just give his solemn promise not to run away and have that be enough to convince

Abby to let him help. More than the loneliness, more than the worry that his farm was going to shit and his dog was slowly wasting away without him – which at least that worry was completely founded – was how rough it was to just be cooped up in a cell all day.

He ran his fingers through Maggie's mangy coat mindlessly as his body filled with restless energy. Day in, day out, to sit in a cell and stare at the same walls and read the same books and eat the same food, with only two chances a day to stretch his legs…it was maddening, especially for someone who was used to being outside most of the day, working in the fields or during the winter, working in the barn. Riding his horse, Elvis, along his fences, checking for breaks.

Anything but just sitting and staring.

Maggie, seemingly sensing his restlessness, began stirring beneath his fingers, and then with a shake of her fur, she jumped off the bed and walked to the cell door, nosing against it and whining.

Wyatt thought for a moment that she'd

been reading his mind and was trying to say she wanted to go be free in the world, and then he realized that rather than an existential crisis about where her life was going, it was much more likely that she just needed to take a leak.

Rolling his eyes at himself, he pushed himself off the bed and rattled the bars of the cell. "Abby! Declan!" he called out, Maggie whining beside him. "I'll get you outside in just a minute," Wyatt promised her, scratching her behind the ears. "They're going to make me come back and pick up all your shit when the snow melts in the spring, you know." As much as Wyatt didn't look forward to the idea, he was still thankful they let her in here to be with him. As awful as it was to be cooped up in his cell all day, having her with him was already giving him some of his sanity back.

Abby hurried down the cell block toward him, her arms filled with blankets and flashlights. Declan trailed behind her with pillows in his arms.

At Wyatt's quizzical look, she said, "No

emergency generator means no heat and no lights. We'll have to make do for tonight."

"Well, Maggie Mae needs a trip outside if you know what I mean," Wyatt said with a wry grin. "Her whines are getting louder by the moment, I swear." She was nudging his leg rather insistently, and Wyatt just patted her re-assuringly. "We'll get you outside, girl."

Abby opened the cell door and stepped to the side. "Go on outside with her. Don't let the door close behind you – it'll lock and you'll be stuck out there until spring. I'll get this set up," she said with a jerk towards their cell.

Wyatt nodded his appreciation, unsure how to tell her how much it meant to him that she wasn't guarding his every move, believing he was about to spring the Great Escape on her. Truthfully, even in the depths of his hatred at the system, he wouldn't have tried to escape. He wanted to go back to his farm and pick up the pieces of his life. Living on the lam for the rest of it just didn't appeal to him. He wasn't going to leave the jail until the county let him go as a free man.

He opened the door to the courtyard, a gush of wind catching the door and yanking his body out into the cold. As Maggie passed him and began hunting through the snowdrifts, looking for just the right place to do her business, Wyatt held onto the door handle with all his might. He'd never been thrown around by wind like this before. He was 6'2" and a whole lot of work muscle. He didn't get pushed around easily.

As he watched Maggie make her circles in the snow, he realized how mundane and boring his life had become before that night at Mr. Petrol's. Plant, harvest, plant, harvest, watch TV or read a book...he'd retreated from the world after Shelly and Sierra had died. He needed to start doing things again; start helping out in the community. He'd heard about Adam Whitaker's special needs camp that he was starting up, and after his help with Maggie, Wyatt wanted to do something to help him out in return.

Plus, he could reintegrate with the world in

a small way. His counselor would be happy to hear him make these plans, that's for sure.

Finally, Maggie Mae found the perfect snowdrift and crouched down. He swore he could hear a happy sigh escape from her as she looked towards him, her tongue lolling happily.

He grinned at her obvious joy at being able to relieve her bladder. Dogs were so simple, so straightforward. They loved you or hated you. There was never any question of what they were thinking, or why. Maybe that was why he'd always been more comfortable working with animals. Dogs, horses, even dumb-as-a-pile-of-rocks cows were all just...them. No artifice, no hiding and lying and distorting the truth. He could count on them to simply be them.

They've never let you down.

And wasn't that just the root of it all.

His wandering thoughts were brought back to the present when he began shivering from the biting cold. Luckily, Maggie had stayed on his side of the courtyard; it wasn't a large area, but he didn't want to have to go searching for her through the blinding snow. It was stinging his eyes, cheeks, and ears, and he was sure his nose was going to turn into a frozen icicle at any moment.

C'mon girl, piss faster…

Finally, she straightened up and after doing a few passes with her nose to make sure everything came out all right, she trotted towards him, her tongue still happily lolling to the side. She didn't seem the least bit thrown off by the massive amount of snow coming down.

She trotted in past him and shook her fur, spraying him and the walls, floor, and ceiling with wet dog hair and frozen snow pellets. "Maggiiieee," Wyatt said with a half-laugh, half-sigh. He'd have to ask Abby for a towel to dry her off, and a mop to clean up the mess.

Maggie looked up at him, recognizing her name, and then when he didn't tell her to go chase cows or round up the chickens, she nudged his hand, obviously reminding him that he hadn't told her what to do.

"What you get to do," he said, stroking her sopping wet head, "is come back to the jail cell with me and get warm. No chickens in here." She licked his hand and then they took off down the cell block and back to his cell.

He couldn't wait to get out of here. Just a couple more weeks and then…freedom. Or, at least probation. Which was a hell of a lot closer to freedom than he had right now.

CHAPTER 12

ABBY

Just as Wyatt and Maggie came around the corner, looking like two lost souls coming in from a trip to Antarctica, the lights flickered for just a moment, and Abby held her breath. *Maybe they'd stay…*

Darkness.

"Really?" Wyatt's voice held exasperation and a hint of laughter. "Declan, I guess we oughta just be happy that this is truly a Christmas we'll never forget."

"I can't imagine we will," Declan said dryly

in the darkness. Maggie didn't seem to think this was nearly as funny as the two Miller brothers did, and she began whining her uncertainty.

Abby fumbled with the flashlight always strapped to her service belt and then flicked it on. The beam shot through the darkness, hindering almost as much as it was helping. "Hold on, let me get back to the other flashlights," she said, and ducked to grab the flashlights lined up underneath Wyatt's bunk. She'd put them there after bringing supplies back to the cell, wanting an easy place to find them in case they were actually needed.

In a snowstorm like this, the county plows would have a hard time getting the roads cleared enough that the Idaho Power electricians would be able to fix the problem, wherever it was at in the valley, and that meant that they weren't likely to get power back until morning, maybe longer. She grabbed a flashlight for each brother and tossed them over, carefully tossing Wyatt's through the bars of the cell. With a flashlight in her master's hand, Maggie's whines died away and she followed him into the cell obediently.

"Do you have a towel for me to dry her?" Wyatt asked, nodding his head towards his mostly frozen dog. Abby pulled two from the stack and tossed them to him also.

"I figured you'd need one after you went outside. Got one for both of you."

He caught them easily and his teeth flashed in the semi-darkness. "Thanks."

His husky voice did something…unmentionable to her stomach and she worked hard to shove that feeling far, far away. She could *not* allow herself to feel anything for Wyatt Miller.

Not

Possible

"So what's the plan?" Wyatt asked the group. "Are there special bunks for officers who have to stay at the jail overnight?"

She shook her head. "Normally, we have a checklist of items that we have to take care of, and we're responsible for working our way down the list. After that, it's a simple matter of keeping a chair from floating away, and staying awake. Someone has to be at the jail at all times if there's a prisoner here, so it's not even like I could go out on patrol, even if the roads were clear. At this point, I'd probably be reading and trying to keep my eyeballs propped open. Luckily, I don't have to work many overnights."

Her incredibly long day – her normal shift combined with this unexpected second shift – was starting to wreak havoc on her body. Whether or not she was actually supposed to sleep on the job was no longer up for debate. She would *have* to sleep tonight. It was simply a matter of deciding where she was going to sleep.

"I think you should sleep in here with us," Declan said, voicing her thoughts out loud. "With the electricity off, I imagine the heat's gone too, right?"

She nodded. "It's a gas furnace, but it relies on electricity to keep the pilot light lit. The back-up generator is supposed to take care of all of that, but…" She shrugged.

"It doesn't make much sense to have you out, wandering around in jail, possibly getting hurt in the dark, and we wouldn't even know it," Wyatt pointed out. "We should stick together. Just for tonight. Come morning, we'll figure out what to do."

She liked the word "we." It implied her and Wyatt together.

She liked it a little too much. She needed to stop liking it, pronto.

Declan settled down into the second bunk in the cell, and Abby realized with a start how weird that felt to her. For six weeks now, the only bunk that had been used in the cell was Wyatt's. The other one stayed untouched. They had six cells with two beds each, so when other people were housed in the jail, Wyatt hadn't had to share. Luckily, the Long Valley County Jail wasn't filled to capacity very often.

But now, just having the other bunk filled felt…off.

And it felt even more off when Wyatt insisted that she sleep in his bunk. "I can sleep on the floor. No woman is going to sleep on the floor while I sleep on a bed." Abby felt like calling these bunks with their squeaky mattresses a "bed" was a real stretch of the imagination, but she finally acquiesced. Arguing and winning with a Miller brother was a feat not many people had managed, and she didn't think it was likely she'd win tonight.

Wyatt settled down into a pile of blankets on the floor, Maggie next to him, and he and Declan began messing around, using the flashlights as spotlights, holding them up underneath their chins and telling ghost stories. Abby laughed at the obvious over-the-top plots and extreme "ghostly voices" that they were using.

Eventually, they began telling childhood stories, stories that Abby noticed didn't include Stetson, at least not in any major way. She tried to remember how many years there were between Wyatt and Stetson. She knew Stetson had been a surprise to the Miller couple, and they'd struggled some with including him with the two older brothers. She wondered if that was at the root of the problems between Wyatt and Stetson, or if it was something else.

Speaking of problems…

Wyatt also stole Daddy's farm out from underneath him just when he needed help, not a kick when he was down.

It was something she didn't like to focus on much; she tried not to let the anger at what Wyatt had said around town afterwards get to her. It was easier for her to let it go than it was for her father, though. He would never forgive Wyatt – not for stealing his farm, nor for bad-mouthing him to anyone who would sit still.

Yet another reason to not let yourself fall in love, Abby.

She wasn't sure if the stern warning was going to be heeded or not. Her mind knew what she should do but her heart was flat-out ignoring logic and reason.

She heard Declan's deep breathing and re-alized he'd fallen asleep. She could hear Maggie's snores ringing out, and wondered if Wyatt was asleep also. How long had she let her thoughts wander?

"Are you asleep?" Wyatt asked, his face popping up on the side of the bed, eyes just an inch from her own. She stifled back a scream at his sudden appearance, and then leaned forward and whacked him across the head.

"Yes, I'm *fully* awake now, thankyouverymuch," she whispered scoldingly. He grinned at her – two smiles in one day! – and then disappeared out of sight again. Abby wriggled to the edge of the bed so she could see what he was doing, hating every squeak of the mattress as she moved. Damn, these things were obnoxious. Why did they curse their inmates with them? By the end of a month, she'd be stark-raving mad if she had to sleep on one every night.

She really should convince her dad to swap them out for something that wasn't quite so obnoxious. Of course, that meant having to explain to her dad that she slept in Wyatt's cell.

She'd rather keep that bit of information to herself.

For this one night, with the blanket of white wrapping around the jail, enclosing them in their own little cocoon, she could ignore the world. She could ignore the fact that she was the jailer, that Wyatt was the prisoner, that she shouldn't be doing what she was doing, that she shouldn't be feeling what she was feeling.

Just for one night. One little Christmas miracle, one little moment of letting go of doing what was strictly correct, and doing instead what felt right.

One night wouldn't hurt her…right?

She peered over the edge of the mattress and saw Wyatt was rearranging his nest of bedding on the floor. "What are you doing?" she asked curiously.

"If I'm going to talk to you since Declan conked out on me and Maggie isn't much for talking, I thought I'd move closer to you. Just so we can talk more quietly and not disturb Dec."

Which is when she said something she never, ever thought she would.

"You should come up here."

Oh my God, Abby, where did that come from?

The lighting in the jail was awful, with the flashlights standing on end, shining straight up at the ceiling, leaving everything else in semi-darkness.

But even in that dark, spooky lighting, she could see him freeze. The world stopped for a moment as he just stared at her. "Are you...are you sure?" he asked tentatively. He wasn't moving an inch; she couldn't even tell if he was breathing. He seemed to have been utterly frozen by the idea.

"It's only going to get colder in here as the heat in the building dissipates," she pointed out reasonably. "You're lying on the cold cement floor. By morning, you could have frostbite."

Except, what she wasn't saying was, Wyatt and Declan should snuggle up in a bunk together, and she and Maggie Mae should snuggle up together. She could stand the dog's awful breath for one night. Probably.

What she absolutely should *not* be doing is snuggling up with Wyatt Miller, the man with a chip on his shoulder the size of Texas. The man who'd beat a guy into a bloody pulp, requiring two rounds of reconstructive surgery to get his nose back into what might reasonably be called decent shape. The man who'd humiliated her father in front of everyone.

The man who made her heart go pitter-patter in her chest.

No, she should *definitely* not snuggle up to him.

Ignoring the best advice she'd ever given herself, she pulled the edge of the blanket back and patted on the thin mattress. Even just this brief exposure to the rapidly cooling air made her shiver. "C'mon, before all the heat gets out," she urged him. He flicked the two flashlights off, plunging the cell into total, disorienting darkness, and then shuffled his way to his bunk, climbing up beside her.

"You face that direction," she said, pointing away from her, and then, realizing he couldn't see her, added, "Away from me. I'll snuggle up to your back so we can keep warm." *And your penis can be facing a different direction than towards me.* Because she was sure that it would want more than what she or Wyatt would think was a good idea.

No matter how good it would feel.

Slowly, haltingly, they began chatting, and he ever-so-slowly relaxed back against her, her arm draped over his muscular chest. She found herself stroking his chest a few times and forced herself to stop each time. It was instinctual but she couldn't let herself do it. It wasn't appropriate, to say the least.

None of this was, but she was ignoring that fact for the moment, and clinging to the idea that she'd do this with anyone under the circumstances. Anyone at all.

She just happened to be a little more willing when it came to Wyatt Miller.

A little lot more willing, to be specific.

"After losing Sierra and Shelly to that asshole, I've felt a huge hole in my life," Wyatt said quietly into the darkness. "I miss my wife; everyone who knew her, loved her. She was a wonderful companion and we got along well, for the most part. I think most people who've been married for a while will tell you that no spouse is perfect, and we certainly had our fights.

"But Sierra? Losing her was to lose a part

of my soul. If I were to ever risk getting married again, risk falling in love with someone, it would be to have kids. I won't have another Sierra, I know that. But I miss her so much. I miss pushing her on the swing set. I miss teaching her how to count and what her colors are and the difference between a circle and an oval. I miss teaching her how to read. My wife was a huge reader; we have books everywhere in our house, but when Sierra was born, we quickly went from reading the farm report and the latest *New York Times* bestsellers, to reading *The Cat in the Hat*. And I didn't mind, not one bit. I would've done anything for my daughter. Anything at all."

His voice died away in the darkness, and Abby heard all that he didn't say but meant, and she felt panic well up inside of her. *No reason to panic, Abby Connelly. There was never anything real between you and Wyatt anyway, and you know it. This is just the last reminder that you need to let it go.*

But instead of wiggling her way over onto her left side, turning away from Wyatt and his body and his warmth and his smell, she snuggled closer instead. Because it was Christmas Eve and if only for one night, she deserved to be happy. To pretend it could all be hers.

Tomorrow would come soon enough.

CHAPTER 13

WYATT

S LOWLY, Wyatt came awake. He was cold, his nose and cheeks and ears feeling frozen, almost frostbitten, but his body was deliciously warm. And comfortable. There was a soft, warm body next to his that smelled so good. Even before he was fully awake, his dick was standing at attention. He wanted to snuggle up against…

Abby Connelly?

He froze, his arm wrapped around her waist, and his eyes staring at her profile, just an inch away from the curve of her ear. He wanted to lean forward and nuzzle her neck. He wanted to kiss his way over to her delightfully pink mouth, open as she breathed in and out softly, dead asleep to the world.

The high windows running the length of the cell block let in a little light, weak and faltering and gray, but there. Enough to know who he was lying next to, enough to know that last night, when she'd invited him to sleep next to her, that it hadn't been a dream.

As cold as it was in the cell, what with his right arm out above the blanket and feeling only slightly warmer than *popsicle*, he knew that her allowing him to sleep next to her kept him warm enough to actually sleep. Lying on the cold cement jail floor, he might've otherwise spent a miserable night shivering, teeth chattering, trying to stay warm, even with Maggie.

He drew his arm down, underneath the blankets, as quietly as he could, trying not to disturb Abby. As much as his mind knew that lying there with her was a Class A *Awful* Idea, his body...it quite liked the idea, to say the least.

He closed his eyes, pretending for just a moment that he was at home, in bed, and it was his wife lying next to him.

It was a dangerous game to play. He shouldn't be playing it. He knew that, without a doubt in his mind.

But that didn't make the temptation any less real. Any less overwhelming.

I think I'm falling in love with Abby Connelly.

He squeezed his eyes as hard as he could, as if to push those words out of his mind.

Even more so than wanting to sleep with her, falling in love with her was a giant no-no, complete with red flashing lights and a siren going a million miles a minute.

Out of all the women in all the world to fall in love with, Abby was the Number One Worst Choice Ever. Her father hated his guts, she was his jailer, and…

And…

Well, he was sure there were more reasons that it wouldn't work between them. He just had to take the time to come up with them.

He searched, flipping through reasons, until

he realized that every one of them were reasons that he was attracted to her. The way she'd laugh until she snorted, and then she'd turn this brilliant, gorgeous pink. How thoughtful she was, even requesting that the diner not put tomatoes on his sandwiches after their discussions on the downright awfulness of raw tomatoes and how they simply weren't fit to be eaten.

And she was gorgeous – absolutely, perfectly, wonderfully gorgeous. She'd been too skinny in high school; too much of a stick for his tastes. He hadn't paid much attention to her back then, because she'd been so much younger than him, and because she just hadn't been his type. He liked women with meat on their bones, not women who he'd crush just by looking at them sideways.

But ever since high school, she'd started to fill out, her curves just right. Her curves, which were currently pressed against him. He stifled a groan. He was going to end up a eunuch if this lasted much longer, or at least wishing he was a eunuch. He only had so much self-control and the little that was there was rapidly disappearing, the longer she lay next to him.

She mumbled in her sleep and his breathing stopped. As torturous as it was to lay next to her, it was even worse to contemplate having her leave. He didn't want her going *anywhere*. At age 66, he would still want to be right there, hoping she would continue to sleep.

But her mumbles got a little louder and then her eyelashes fluttered open. Her lips curled softly into a drowsy smile…

Right before it hit her.

She shot up in bed, clutching the blankets to her chest as she went. Wyatt instantly shivered from the blast of freezing cold air that hit him.

"Hi. Good morning. I'm getting out of bed now. Sorry to disturb you. I'm leaving. Good day."

Throughout that barrage of words, she was trying to wiggle over him without actually touching him in the most awkward horizontal mambo in the history of mankind. She got to the edge of the bed and tumbled off, hair flying through the air as she landed with a loud thump on the floor. Maggie Mae, who'd curled up in the nest of blankets that Wyatt had left on the floor, stood up with a stretch and then nosed her new companion on the floor, taking a swipe at Abby's nose and mouth in greeting.

"Hi, Maggie," Abby said, clearly not comfortable at all, while also still being about 52% asleep. "I need to go and I need to do stuff. Important stuff. Official stuff." She scrambled to her feet, her wrinkled uniform in a disarray, and Wyatt was sure, for just a moment, that he'd spotted a red lacy bra before she straightened her shirt out.

"You need any help with that important, official stuff?" Declan asked dryly. She whirled around, her hand on her chest. She obviously hadn't realized Declan was awake any more than Wyatt had.

"Sure. Yes. That'd be great. I'll be upfront. I'll meet you when you're ready," she said, scooping up her service belt on her way out of the cell. She left the door slightly open so Declan could get out without a problem and headed up front without looking back.

Declan looked at Wyatt, then at the floor, then back at Wyatt again.

"Wanna tell me about the sleeping arrangements last night?" he asked.

"Nope."

"Didn't think so."

Wyatt and Declan both slid out of their warm bunks and into the freezing cold air. Wyatt threw on his shoes and wrapped his blanket around himself as Declan got dressed for the day.

"Hey Wyatt?" Declan said as Wyatt paused at the door of the cell, ready to let Maggie out into the courtyard for a morning bathroom run.

"Yeah?"

"Merry Christmas. Maybe next one will be better."

"Thanks. You, too."

Except as Wyatt walked with Maggie to the courtyard door, careful not to let the door swing shut behind him, he couldn't help thinking that his Christmas morning hadn't been too shabby.

CHAPTER 14

ABBY

*J*ANUARY 3RD. After all of the waiting, the day had finally come. Thankfully, the roads to Boise had long ago been cleared after the Storm of the Century had raged through the valley, and they'd be able to make it there today. They could do a video linkup with Ada County if they had to, but that was always so awkward. People didn't really feel like they'd had their day in court if they spent that day in a conference room instead.

Abby looked at the schedule. Officer Rios should be coming in off patrols soon, which meant he could be the second officer required for the transportation of prisoners. Not that Wyatt was going to attack her and make a run for it, but it was official policy that two officers do a transport so that an officer was never left alone with a prisoner.

Of course, in her and Wyatt's case, that was a good thing, not because Wyatt was going to run for the hills or Abby was going to shoot him, but because then at least they could be sure they wouldn't kiss.

Because if they were in danger of doing anything, it was setting the sheets on fire with all of the sparks shooting off them. Something she really, really couldn't allow herself to focus on, at least not while at work.

"Abby, I'm going to be coming with you today."

Her father's booming voice broke her out of her thoughts, and it took a moment for her to realize what he'd said.

"What?" she asked dumbly, taken aback by his words. Surely her dad wouldn't be coming on a transport. As the sheriff, he simply wasn't involved in the day-to-day activities, like transporting prisoners to other counties. She couldn't remember the last time he'd gone out on a prisoner transport. Probably not since the day they pinned that sheriff's badge to his chest.

"I've been cooped up in my office for too long. Time to stretch my legs and get outside," her dad said with a fake, jovial smile.

Stretch his legs…by getting into a cop car for 90 minutes? Fresh air? It was bullshit, plain and simple. She simply arched her eyebrow at him and crossed her arms over her chest. She didn't say a word, and she didn't have to.

He scowled.

"Don't look at me like that. It's nothing personal. I just want to get out of my office for the day."

"Uh-huh," she said, the sarcasm dripping off each syllable like honey off a wooden spoon. "Okay, Sheriff." As the sheriff, she couldn't tell him what to do, and she knew it, and he knew that she knew it. And he was taking advantage of that fact, and they both knew that.

"Go ahead and get the prisoner ready," her dad said, brushing her off. She sighed and headed for the back. It was going to be a long-ass day. Her father and Wyatt in a cop car for an hour and a half, both ways?

She might end up breaking up more than one fistfight today.

When she came walking up to the cell door, Wyatt was already standing there, a big smile on his face.

"Today's the day," he said, the happiness threading through his voice. This was the happiest she'd heard him since the day Declan had brought Maggie into the jailhouse. Speaking of…

"You should probably take Maggie outside for a quick potty break before we leave," she said, gesturing towards the snoring Maggie on the floor. "Otherwise, it's going to be a long day for her." It was already going to be a long day for everyone else; it wasn't right to torture the dog, too. She wasn't looking forward to seeing

Wyatt's face when he realized that he was going to be stuck in a cop car for hours on end with her father.

Wyatt flashed her a grateful smile. "Thanks, we appreciate it. C'mon girl, let's go outside." Instantly awake, Maggie stood up and shook out her coat, trotting over to the jail door. Abby unlocked it and swung it open, giving Maggie her mandatory pettings before letting them both out into the jail yard for a walk around and a pee break. Wyatt sent her another grateful smile as he walked past her, and the butterflies in her stomach went crazy, wilder than a bronco in a rodeo.

Yup, a long day for sure, between a father who wanted to kill, and a prisoner who wanted to kiss.

They made their way through the winding valley towards Boise, the river below only partially frozen over because of the speed and strength of the water flow, pine trees dusted with snow bending over the road above.

It was a drive that Abby loved to take; most people in Long Valley dreaded the drive to

Boise because of the hairpin turns and the much-too-skinny bridges that spanned the river every time the road crossed over it. Abby loved the views, though – the glimpses through the trees up into the endless blue skies, the rushing water over tumbling rocks below…it was wild and free.

Everything that Abby was not.

They got to the Ada County Courthouse and Abby helped Wyatt out of the car, holding his elbow as they walked towards the back entrance and into the courthouse. Her father walked along beside them, harrumphing as they went. He seemed upset by everything today – she was driving too fast. Too slow. Passing too many cars. Not passing enough cars. Her normally peaceful and gorgeous drive to Boise had been anything but. She was just happy to have finally gotten to stable ground, where she wouldn't be told, "Stop riding the break so much."

Backseat drivers (or passenger seat drivers, to be completely accurate) were the worst, especially when they came in the form of her father, the sheriff, and her boss, all rolled up into one.

Wyatt shot her a weak smile and she realized that he was as nervous as a long-tailed cat in a room full of rocking chairs. She smiled back, putting all of the warmth she could fit into the gesture. She gave a gentle squeeze on his elbow, which was as much as she dared to do with her father breathing down their necks, but he gave an answering smile back, and she knew he realized she was on his side, even if it sometimes felt like the rest of the world wasn't.

The clerk at the counter got them checked in and registered, then sent them down the hallway and to the left, to the courtrooms. They were seated in the back to await his turn, but unlike that day in the Long Valley courtroom, this judge was quick to call Wyatt's name. He moved forward into the defendant's area, meeting with his lawyer for a quick whispered discussion, as Abby and the sheriff moved to the front pews reserved for the audience.

C'mon, Judge, don't be a jackass. See the man in

front of you. She sent up a plea to anyone and everyone who might be listening. If there was someone who deserved another chance to do the right thing, it was Wyatt Miller.

Then they did something Abby had heard of but had never witnessed – they swore in the whole courtroom. All of the audience, the prosecutor, the defendant, all in one fell swoop. Everyone was told that they were swearing to tell the truth, rather than making the audience say it in tandem with each other, and Abby had to smile to herself. Very efficient courtroom. So different from Long Valley County, where old traditions die hard.

The prosecutor stood up – a lawyer assigned to the case from Ada County, it was clear from the start that he just didn't care about it. "Your Honor, Wyatt Mister—"

"—Miller," Wyatt's lawyer said, interrupting.

"Oh yes," the prosecutor said, pulling the paper closer to his face to peer at it, "Wyatt Miller beat a gentleman up at a convenience store in an effort to stop the man from driving drunk. He's since spent seven weeks in jail. I think he's done his time and I move to drop all charges against him."

Abby's eyebrows shot up, as did everyone else's in the courtroom. If she'd sat down and tried to imagine the words that would come out of the prosecutor's mouth as part of his opening statement, she would've guessed a hundred other scenarios before she imagined this one. Chaos broke out in the courtroom as people began whispering to each other and Abby felt her father's shoulders tighten up.

He was pissed.

"Your Honor!" he said, shooting to his feet, anger vibrating in his voice.

The judge began banging his gavel. "Order in the court!" he practically shouted over the noise. The audience settled down, but her father remained standing. Abby looked around the courtroom, not recognizing anyone there except Wyatt and his lawyer, of course. The rest of the people must all be waiting for their turn to be heard, and thus had no stake in the situation. She wondered how often the Ada

County prosecutor suggested that the defendant simply be let free. She was guessing not very often.

"Your Honor," her father said again as soon as the noise level died down, "I protest! This is not the first time that Wyatt Miller," he sneered the last name, "has beaten up someone who got in his way. He's assaulted an officer of the law — me! I demand that he be punished for his actions. He cannot act as a one-man vigilante, beating up anyone who he deems deserves it. That's no way to run a town and I won't let it happen in mine!"

The judge just stared at the sheriff for a long moment, and the noise level in the courtroom dropped to dead silence. And still, he continued staring. The sheriff started shifting from foot to foot, unsure of what to say or do. "Your Hon—" he finally started up again but the judge held up his hand, stopping him.

"Mr. Miller," he said, turning toward Wyatt, "at the beginning of this hearing, everyone was sworn in, including you. Would you be willing to waive your Fifth Amendment rights and stand up and answer some questions?"

Wyatt's lawyer leaned over and began whispering in Wyatt's ear, but Wyatt waved him away and stood up. "I would, Your Honor."

The judge nodded gravely.

"Tell me what happened the night that you assaulted our sheriff over there," he said with a jerk of his head towards her father. Her father flinched and she could practically see him biting his tongue, trying to keep his temper. He wasn't used to people dismissing him so easily and it rankled. Hard.

Abby knew that the judge saw right through him, and realized that he wasn't an unbiased bystander in the situation. Obviously, he didn't know anything about the rumors around town or Wyatt buying the Connelly family farm off the auction block after it was foreclosed on or any of the rest of their awful history together, but he knew enough to know that her father wasn't going to give Wyatt a fair shake.

It was strangely comforting to find an outsider who saw the situation the same way that

Abby did. In a small town that acted like an echo chamber so much of the time, looking at a citizen differently than everyone else tended to make a person start to question their sanity after a time.

"I came home from a long day in the fields," Wyatt said, his voice even. "I was exhausted and just wanted to go to bed. My wife needed milk for breakfast the next day, and asked me to go buy it. She'd had a rough day with our daughter, and had just wanted me to go take care of this for her." His voice started to waiver a little and Abby could feel the pain rolling off him in waves.

"I told her no, that I was going to go to bed. Told her to take Sierra, our daughter, and go to the store to get the damn milk, that I was too tired to watch her while my wife was gone. She was angry with me, and they left together. I never saw them again." His voice cracked completely, and he had to stop for a minute, until he could gather his composure. "I was asleep when the knock on the door happened. On their way back from Franklin, a drunk driver hit them head-on. I drove to the scene and I wanted to see them. I wanted to tell them how sorry I was, and how much I loved them." His voice cracked again and his jaw trembled as he tried to gain control. Abby wanted to run to his side, slip her hand in his and tell him that it was going to be okay, but would it? They would never come back.

How could it be okay?

"The first responders were working on them, trying to resuscitate them, and I came running up in the middle of it. I shouldn't have because I was just getting in the way, but that night…I wasn't thinking clearly. The sheriff grabbed me and pulled me away, telling me I had to leave them alone and I took a swing at him."

"He knocked me on my ass and damn near broke my jaw!" the sheriff broke in, anger pouring out of him. "I ended up having to—"

"Enough!" the judge roared. "If you interrupt these proceedings one more time, Sheriff Connelly, I'll have you arrested for contempt of court! You may sit down." He glared at her father over the half-moon of his glasses, the "request" no request at all, but a direct order.

Her father sank down beside her on the bench, muttering under his breath. Abby tried hard to block his words out. Whatever he was saying, she wasn't going to agree with him on it, so it was best if she just ignored him. He'd calm down…eventually.

"You may continue," the judge said to Wyatt.

Wyatt nodded and said, "He's right. I did knock him backwards. I didn't meant to, but I was wild with grief and not paying much attention to what I was doing. I was simply trying to get to my babies." He shrugged. "I was arrested for assaulting an officer but the prosecuting attorney in Long Valley County refused to press charges against me. My wife and daughter died that night, on the side of the road. I guess the prosecutor figured I'd been punished enough."

"What happened on the evening of November 13th, outside of Mr. Petrol's convenience store?" the judge asked.

"It was my wife's brother. He and I had never been best buddies, but after my wife and daughter died, he decided to blame me for their deaths. I'm not entirely sure he's wrong, because I made them drive to Franklin when I should've been the one to do it." He swallowed hard and the lump in Abby's throat only grew. Surely, after all this time, he didn't still blame himself for his wife and daughter's death. Surely he realized that accidents happen, and it was the fault of the drunk driver.

It was the second wreck the driver had caused while being intoxicated, and he was driving without a license when it happened. The drunk driver was the kind of person who should be locked up, the key just thrown away.

Not Wyatt. He was rough and spiky and testy, sure, but he was also loving and loyal and a damn hard worker.

He continued, interrupting her wandering thoughts. "When he pulled up that night at the convenience store, I thought he was going to take out the plate glass windows. He skidded in much too fast and only just stopped in time."

"Did you know who it was when he pulled in?" the judge asked.

"Yes, Your Honor. He drives an orange camo Jeep. There are only so many of those in the Long Valley area." He gave a little smile at that.

The judge nodded. "Go on."

"Well, he came in and bought a 24-pack of Bud Light. The clerk let him because his probation was almost up, and he didn't want to piss off the judge's son. I believe Dick knew that, and took full advantage of the situation. I went outside to tell him to not drive drunk, when he called me 'Killer.'"

The whole courtroom gasped, even her father. Abby felt like someone had punched her in the gut. Holy cow. Richard was lucky he was still alive. Somehow, in all of the rumors that had swirled around about the altercation that night, no one had mentioned that part.

"That's when I pulled him out of the Jeep and started swinging."

The judge nodded slowly, thoughtfully. "Am

I to understand that you've been undergoing counseling since this happened?"

"Yes, Your Honor. I've been seeing a counselor twice a week. She comes to the jail and we talk."

"Well son, you need to realize that you can't keep punching your way through life." Her father harrumphed next to her, pleased to hear that the judge was finally seeing reason. "However, you've also served much more of a jail sentence than you ever should have, under the circumstances, something our fine prosecutor here seems to have realized."

The prosecutor jerked his head up, surprised to have been brought into the conversation. Abby hid her smile. The man had promptly stopped paying any attention to the proceedings, as soon as the judge asked Wyatt to stand, and had instead been shuffling through papers and making notes. She was pretty sure that the paperwork in front of the man had nothing to do with Wyatt. In the largest county in the state of Idaho, she was sure that a brawl outside of a convenience store ranked just above "jaywalker" on his list of things to worry about, and it showed.

"Yes, I agree," the prosecutor said, jumping to his feet. The judge waved him away and the man gratefully sat back down and got back to work. Her father's harrumphs promptly turned…less genial and if they hadn't been in the courtroom, she was sure he would've given the lawyer a piece of his mind.

"I hereby sentence you to three counseling appointments per week for three weeks, and 75 hours of community service. Perhaps you can learn to start solving your problems with something else other than your fists."

"Yes, Your Honor," Wyatt said.

"Now, we need to discuss the terms of your community service. You'll need to drive here to Boise so you can check in with our probation officers – how far of a drive is it from Sawyer?"

"It's 90 minutes, Your Honor," his lawyer said. "Through a narrow canyon."

The judge's eyebrows drew together. "Certainly not ideal during the wintertime," he mumbled. "Unless we can find someone local to handle your probation, however, I don't see a way around it—"

"I'll do it!"

The words were flying out of Abby's mouth before she could stop them. She found herself on her feet, grasping onto the bench in front of her. The judge shot her a puzzled look. "And who are you?" he asked, not unkindly.

"Officer Abby Connelly from Long Valley County," she said.

"Is this your father?" he asked, jerking his head towards the sheriff. She could practically feel the anger rolling off her father, threatening to set her on fire with the strength of it.

"Yes, Your Honor." *If he doesn't disown me by sundown, that is.*

"Well, I accept your offer. Seventy-five hours of community service, with Officer Connelly as the probation officer, and counseling sessions. Hearing dismissed!" He banged his gavel and just like that, the hearing was over. Abby was surprised by the abruptness of the dismissal, but she quickly gained her bearings and hurried over to Wyatt before her father could drag her outside by the scruff of her neck and pitch her into a snowbank.

Wyatt was discussing something in low tones with his lawyer but at her approach, he looked up and grinned, the relief writ large all over his face.

She grinned back, and the feeling of relief washed over her again. She may've just pissed her father off for life, but she didn't care. She'd done the right thing, and that was all that mattered.

CHAPTER 15

WYATT

W HEN ABBY CAME walking toward him, Wyatt couldn't hide the giant grin threatening to split his face. When the judge had started talking about having him do his community service in Boise, his stomach had dropped to the floor. They'd been lucky today to have clear roads the whole way through. More than a few people died on the trip from Sawyer to Boise because of black ice, avalanches, or treacherous conditions that sent them spinning off the side of the road. Many people in Long Valley owned two or three chest freezers so they could stock up on food to minimize the needed trips to Boise during the winter. He would've hated having to make the trip every week for weeks on end.

But now…

Abby grinned back at him, obviously just as happy with the judge's ruling as he was. He held out his wrists and with a huge grin, she unlocked them, pulling the metal away from his wrists and hooking the handcuffs back on her belt. They shared an unspoken victorious smile, and then they headed back out into the wintry day, the icy wind piercing his skin almost immediately, but it didn't matter. Nothing could bother him now, not even sub-zero temperatures.

Sheriff Connelly followed along behind them, and Wyatt knew that he was in for a hell of a car ride home. The sheriff was going to be as excited about what happened in the courtroom as he would be to have his home set ablaze, but Wyatt couldn't exactly find much pity in his soul for him.

He'd tried, once, to tell the sheriff the truth about the rumors that had swirled around town, but the sheriff had brushed him off, and quite frankly, Wyatt wasn't the kind of person to beg for another's time twice. If the sheriff didn't want to listen to him, Wyatt wasn't about to wrestle him to the ground and force him to.

They got into the car, Wyatt still in the back of course, but this time, without his hands cuffed in front of him. He stared down wonderingly at his hands. Freedom. Sure, he still had his community service to do, and yes, he still had his counseling appointments to go to, but he could take Maggie and he could go home. To his own bed.

Nothing sounded more heavenly at the moment than that.

As they followed the road back out of town and back into the hairpin turns of the canyon between Boise and Sawyer, he started to think about his community service. Sure, Abby was going to be his probation officer, but what was he going to do on his probation?

He couldn't imagine stamping books in and out at the library, and it wasn't like he could do a landscaping project for a local organization in the dead of winter. He could shovel snow every week for the Senior Citizen's Center so they could get people in and out for bingo night, but as soon as he thought of it, he dismissed it. This was Long Valley. They would already have someone to shovel snow; they didn't need him. He wanted to do something that mattered with his 75 hours.

Which was when he sat back with a huge grin on his face. Of course. Adam Whitaker. That should've been his first thought. Adam, or Vet Whitaker, was one of his closer friends, outside of Declan of course. If Wyatt had to choose a person to call a friend who wasn't also a relative, Adam was it.

He'd started up a therapy camp for children with special needs and foster children. They worked with horses, learning how to saddle, bridle, brush, and love them. Adam had been smart and picked the gentlest horses this side of the Mississippi, so when one of the children got over-exuberant, the horses stood still for it all. The camp was still in its infancy, and he was sure Adam could use his help with it. Here was something that really mattered.

Wyatt settled back in his seat with a big grin on his face. He hadn't expected to come up with a genius idea so quickly. He just had to ask Adam if he'd be willing to sign off on all of the paperwork, and he'd be set to go.

The smile faded from his face. He was going to have to ask Adam to sign off on all his paperwork. The idea was damn embarrassing. He hated admitting that he was even on probation, let alone having to ask someone like Adam to do his paperwork for him.

With an inward groan, he stared out the window at the passing pine trees. He was being an idiot. While he'd been stuck in jail all those endless weeks, he'd been able to pretend to himself that no one knew about him and what had happened. He was isolated from the Long Valley community, and considering he wasn't exactly a socialite to begin with, he had been perfectly happy to stick his head in the sand and ignore the outside world.

But the chances of no one outside of Abby

and the rest of the county employees knowing what happened that night at the convenience store was about -2.73%.

Everyone knew, and had probably been dining out on the gossip for months now.

Also, if he had to ask someone to sign off on his paperwork, why not make it Adam? At least Adam wouldn't be sending him judgmental glances through it all, tsking about how Wyatt just couldn't control his temper.

No, Adam would ignore it all, and just be happy for the extra set of hands. He was as low-key and drama-free as they came.

Which was exactly why they got along so well.

He was just gonna have to learn how to swallow his pride a little, and ask for some help along the way. It might kill him, but he'd do it.

The sheriff was continuing to make as many comments about Abby's driving on the way back home as he had on the way to Boise. Watching the two of them in action, Wyatt realized that Abby had enough patience for six saints, because if he'd been nitpicked to death by a backseat driver like that, he'd have pulled over and booted the person out of the car, boss or no boss. Father or no father. He just didn't have the patience for those kinds of shenanigans.

About the fifth time that Sheriff Connelly snapped at her for riding the brake too much, Wyatt found himself grinding his back teeth. He didn't figure it'd do to get in a fight with an officer of the law just hours after a hearing about getting into a fight with the son of a judge, but this whole ride was surely testing his patience to the max.

He thought back to what his counselor, Rhonda, had told him. "You can't change what others do, only your reaction to what they do." Which was the kind of mumbo-jumbo bullshit that he hated to hear, but he still tried to figure out what she'd want him to do under the circumstances. Obviously whacking the sheriff upside the head and telling him to quit being a jackass was off the table.

So was saying anything, even politely. The

sheriff wouldn't take to being told what to do by a lowly citizen of the county.

I can change the conversation topic.

Of course. It seemed obvious once he thought about it, but in his defense, this was the first time he'd attempted something like this. He'd admit this out loud about the same time he gave up farming, but there just might be some truth to the idea that he tended to solve his problems with his fists, not his mouth.

"So what news did I miss in the Valley while I was on my vacation?" Wyatt asked through the metal grid separating him from the Connellys up front. "Anyone have a baby or get hitched over Christmas break?"

The sheriff ignored the question, clearly thinking that Wyatt had lost it for wanting to catch up on the local gossip, but Abby was game, and started listing off all of the births, divorces, and marriages of the last couple of months. As they chatted, the sheriff's shoulders eventually loosened just a little and he even smiled and nodded a bit.

Wyatt couldn't wait to tell Rhonda about the progress. She'd be thrilled.

They pulled into town just as the sun was setting in the west, darkness settling over the valley abnormally early, just like it did throughout the winter. Because Sawyer was set in a long valley between two parallel rows of mountains marching into the distance, the short winter days were even shorter, as the sun sank behind the tall mountains, blocking the weak light that would've otherwise filtered through. Long Valley had almost endless twilights because of the mountain ranges, but Wyatt wouldn't have it any other way. These mountains told him that he was home. There was no other place in the world as beautiful, he was sure of it.

Finally pulling into a parking spot behind the courthouse, they all got out and stretched, and then shuffled inside. The sheriff disappeared into his office while Abby completed his release paperwork and Wyatt gathered his few possessions from his cell, leaving his hated striped pajamas behind. With a big grin, he walked back up the cell block, Maggie by his side, tail fanning the air as they went. She couldn't possibly know what was going on, but she could tell when he was happy, and right then, he was just about radiating happiness.

With a nod of farewell to Abby, he stepped out into the weak winter twilight, growing darker by the moment, and then stopped. He had no way home. He hadn't thought to ask Declan to come pick him up, and after he'd been arrested at the convenience store, Declan had arranged to get his pickup back to his farm. Which was six miles outside of town, and he was in no condition to hoof it. When he'd been arrested seven weeks earlier, it'd been much warmer and he'd arrived with only a light fall jacket on his back.

Maggie, happy to be outside – truly outside – for the first time in weeks, was busy marking every tree and bush and snow pile in sight. She'd filled out since they'd first brought her to his cell; her hip bones weren't sticking out as far, and her coat was a lot thicker and shinier.

Not that she was in any shape to walk six miles in the wintry darkness either.

With a sigh, he decided to head across the street and ask to use their phone at the diner. He didn't want to go back inside and admit to Abby that he hadn't considered how he was going to get home; she would think him a true idiot. He'd just fake it and make it home. Somehow.

Just then, the front door of the sheriff's office opened up and out stepped Abby. "Hey, we forgot to arrange for you to get a ride home," she said, her breath coming out in puffs. "Let me just swing you out there myself."

Wyatt's shoulders immediately relaxed. He hated to admit that she was right, but on the other hand, it wasn't exactly like he could hide it from her. He realized then that it was futile to even try. He'd been under lock and key for months now. When, exactly, was he supposed to have made a phone call without her or someone else noticing?

He gave a short nod. "Thanks."

He realized that this was another instance

of him having to swallow his pride. Damn, it was starting to get painful, this pride-swallowing thing. The sooner he could stop relying on others, the better.

"Let me grab the keys for the cruiser. Be right back." She stepped into the sheriff's office, the light spilling out from the glass door growing brighter as the valley sank into the winter night. Maggie ran over to him, finally having marked every tree and bush and interesting object in sight, some of them twice, and was obviously pleased with herself for her industriousness.

"You're such a boy sometimes," he told her with a scratch of her head. She just panted happily, leaning against him as they waited. He knew Maggie had struggled being locked up in a cell day after day with nothing to do – she was a work dog, not a pampered pet. But the other choice had been to send her back to his place without him, and that would've just started the whole cycle all over again.

Plus, these last few weeks, having her there

in the cell with him…it'd made things just that much more bearable. Between her and Abby…

Abby reappeared, keys in hand. "Ready?" she asked rhetorically, and they headed to the back towards the cruiser.

It was time to go home.

CHAPTER 16

ABBY

IT WAS A LITTLE CRAZY, getting into her police car, and having Wyatt get upfront next to her, like he was just some passenger, some citizen needing a ride somewhere. Nothing, really, had changed from just an hour before on the way home from Boise, but the simple act of having him climb in upfront, with no handcuffs on…

Everything had changed.

She scrambled for something to say as they pulled out of the parking lot, Maggie's panting breath the only sound in the winter night. "Have you thought about what you want to do for your community service?" she asked, heading out towards Wyatt's place. Her childhood home. She hadn't been out there since her father had lost it to the bank, and a small part of her wondered how she'd handle the memories sure to come back.

"Yeah. I have to talk to him, of course, but I'm thinking about Adam Whitaker and that new therapy camp of his. I figure he could use another set of hands to help out, especially a pair that knows something about horses."

Abby shot him a big smile. "That's a brilliant idea," she said. "I should've thought about that but it didn't even cross my mind. I'm sure he'd appreciate the help."

Wyatt smiled back and the butterflies began swarming in her stomach, all trying to tell her just how sexy he was.

Not that she needed a reminder. Wyatt was damn sexy, and there was no forgetting that fact any time soon.

There was also the simple fact that her father would approve of them dating...never, as a matter of fact. And there was no getting around that.

"Well, come on over to the courthouse and fill out the paperwork after you've talked to Adam. We can get you started right away on it so you can wrap this up and move on."

The headlights of the car cut through the darkness, lighting the way, while the dashboard lights gave a faint green glow to Wyatt's face, but still, she could see the smile that lit up his face. "That's going to be a great day," he agreed.

Today had been a great day, that was for sure. To finally have a judge who listened and saw Wyatt for who he was, warts and all, rather than through the haze of hatred and blame. The judge and his son wanted to blame someone, anyone, for Shelly's death. Sure, they could blame the drunk driver, but he was from Boise, up in the area on vacation. They didn't know him.

And from what Abby had heard around town, the judge had never really welcomed Wyatt into the family. He'd thought his little girl was too good for him, and hadn't tried to hide that fact from Wyatt, Shelly, or anyone else. It must've been hard to be a part of that family for years, and even harder when she'd died and the people he should've been able to grieve with were the ones who were shunning him and making his life damn miserable.

Yeah, he shouldn't have sent Richard to the hospital; Abby didn't think anyone would dispute that, not even Wyatt. But she understood why it'd happened. Out of all of the people in the world to know that you shouldn't drink and drive, Richard should be it. Thank heavens his Jeep was that awful orange camo color. Everyone knew to dive for cover when he came tearing down the road.

Just then, her childhood home came into view and she switched off the engine with a grin. "You painted the house green," she said with surprise in her voice. Growing up, it'd been stark white. Now a light sage color, she was surprised by how much it changed the look of the house. She could just spot her old bedroom window through the wintry darkness.

"Yeah, Shelly wanted to give it some color," Wyatt said with a shrug. It was obvious, and not surprising, that Wyatt didn't seem to care much about decorating choices. "Thanks for the ride home. Much appreciated." He swung out of the car and opened up the backdoor. "C'mon girl, let's go home," he said, as Maggie streaked out past him and began zigzagging through the dark, reacquainting herself with every rock, snow drift, and tree in the yard. Her tail was going a million miles a minute, and Abby figured that no dog in the history of the world was as happy as Maggie was just then.

With a wave, she turned and headed back down the long, rutted driveway that connected to the county road. The driveway was clear of snow, which meant that Jorge must've been keeping up on the job while Wyatt was in jail. Hopefully he kept up on other chores, too, and Wyatt's farm hadn't fallen into too much disrepair.

It was only a little after five when Abby pulled back onto the smooth blacktop of the county road, but it felt like midnight. It'd been a day. A really wonderful day, but a long day nonetheless.

It was time to go home, take a long bath, and relax. And time to start forgetting about Wyatt Miller and his brilliant blue eyes.

She could start right then.

CHAPTER 17

WYATT

E WALKED INTO the dark house, not bothering to unlock the front door – he hadn't locked it before he'd left that day for the store, and sure enough, no one else had bothered to come along and lock it for him while he'd been in jail.

Even before his hand could find the light switch and turn on the lights, though, his nose was telling him about something else that no one had bothered to do while he was gone: Empty the trash. The stench was overwhelming, almost to the point of making him instantly nauseous, and Maggie whined, immediately did a U-turn, and scratched at the door to be let out.

Wyatt chuckled. He couldn't say as he could blame her. He opened the door and she shot back outside, into the darkness and away from the stench. He smiled for a moment into the January night. If he'd been able to run away from the smell, he would've followed her.

Instead, he propped the front door open and moved through the house, flipping on lights as he went, until he got to the kitchen where the smell was the strongest.

With a sigh, he tackled the biggest problem first – the trashcan. He carried it outside without even opening the lid. He didn't know and he didn't care. He'd buy a new trashcan the next morning. This one was going into the dumpster whole.

Oh dammit, the fridge too. It wasn't just his trash – it was every single bit of fresh food that he'd owned that night of the fistfight. The apples in the bowl on the counter were a mushy brown sludge that turned his stomach just to look at.

This was gonna be fun.

The bowl of apples, curdled milk, rotten sour cream, and a green brick he supposed used to be cheese followed.

Item after item, trip after trip, even to the two bathrooms in the house to empty out those trashcans, until finally, every rotten item in the house had been thrown away. He could only be glad that he'd been incarcerated during the colder parts of the year. If all of that food had sat in the summer heat instead...

He imagined he would've just burnt the house to the ground and started over again.

As it was, he was going to have to pull out his winter gear and sleep on the three-season porch that night. They were definitely in the fourth season of the year and he really shouldn't be sleeping there, but there was no way to get a goodnight's sleep with the lingering odor wafting through the air. He'd call a cleaning company first thing in the morning and beg them to come clean right away. He'd probably have to pay double for their services, but he didn't give a damn.

Anything to have a house that didn't smell like an enclosed garbage dump.

Except…his stomach rumbled. As much as the rotten food had turned his stomach, he'd also worked up a sweat cleaning everything out. He couldn't believe what awful shape he was in. Months of enforced inactivity had kicked his ass. The county jail didn't have an exercise room, only a courtyard that he got to walk around twice a day.

They just didn't house that many long-term prisoners. He was probably the person who'd stayed the longest at the Long Valley County Jail in the last ten years. They usually shipped people off to another county if they were going to be incarcerated for longer than a week or two. He had to wonder if that was the sheriff's doing – that he didn't want to have Wyatt shipped somewhere else as "proof" that he couldn't handle having Wyatt in his jail.

That sounded like the sheriff.

Well, nothing to be done for it. The only

edible food still left in his house were green beans and baked beans, and despite their similarities in names, he wasn't about to dump them both into a saucepan and eat them together. Which meant – he checked his watch – he'd better hurry over to the grocery store if he was going to get there before they closed at nine. Otherwise, he'd be stuck grocery shopping at the convenience store again, and wasn't that what got him into this trouble in the first place?

With a groan, he grabbed his keys and headed out. It was going to be a long night; driving to go buy the food – and maybe a clothespin for his nose while he was at it – coming back and cooking it, then sleeping outside on the porch.

Not exactly the homecoming he'd been envisioning the last few months.

Maggie followed alongside as he headed to his truck, and jumped into the bed, tail wagging. Hot damn, he better buy her dog food, too. Her food was probably at Declan's house, since he'd been trying to take care of her while he was in jail. Dog food at the Shop 'N Go was going to cost an arm and a leg.

Nope, this homecoming wasn't going one bit like he'd been dreaming the past few months.

CHAPTER 18

ABBY

SHE STUDIED THE SHELF in front of her. Bubba's Honey-Sweet BBQ or Mesquite…She'd been standing there for five minutes, trying to decide, and finally with a sigh, threw them both into her cart. When in doubt, buy them both? Sure, why not.

She'd gone home after her shift ended and had changed into civvies, when she realized that she had no food for dinner. Of course.

She was tired beyond words, but out to the Shop 'N Go she'd gone. She could pick up a few items, cook dinner, and *then* take that bubble bath she'd been promising herself.

She pushed her little cart around the corner. Just one more—

Crash!

Her cart went skittering sideways and she fell over, right into…

"Uh…hi Wyatt," she croaked, staring up at him. He looked sweaty and tired and smelled a little bit like…garbage?

She jerked away, upright, onto her own two feet. Even tired, sweaty, and smelling like garbage, her skin sizzled where his hands had touched her arms. She needed to keep her distance. She was his parole officer, dammit. "Out shopping for groceries?" she asked, and immediately wished she could shove her police-issued boots down her own throat. That was just about the most dumbass thing to ask ever. What, exactly, does a person do in a grocery store if it wasn't grocery shopping?

He grinned at her, his face suddenly a lot happier than it'd been when they'd first crashed together. She smiled back. Wyatt smiling was a sight to behold, and it surely didn't do anything for the twerking butterflies in her stomach.

"Yeah, I didn't think about it and apparently no one else did either, but my groceries at my house didn't exactly keep for the last two months."

Her mouth made a perfectly round "O." "Of course," she breathed. "Oh man, I bet your house smelled something fierce when you got home." Which explained the garbage smell.

"I can't say it's the most pleasant smell I've ever come across in my life," he said with a small grin. "Maggie came inside, took one whiff, and turned right back around and wanted out. If I thought that running away would make the situation better, I would've followed right behind her."

"You got it all cleaned out, then?"

"Best I could." He shrugged. "All I had left to eat was beans – baked beans and green beans. Even I knew better than to throw those two into a pot together."

She shuddered. "Yeah, probably not. You want to come to my house for dinner?"

She didn't know where the words had come from. Her jaw was moving and words were coming out and she felt like a total jackass because she couldn't invite him to dinner. She was his probation officer. She absolutely, positively could not invite him to dinner.

And yet? She had.

And she desperately wanted him to say yes, stinky garbage smell and all.

"Yes," he said, his eyes lighting up like she'd just offered him the best present a person could receive. "I'd love that! Let me buy dinner – I was going to go old school and just buy steak and potatoes and some salad. Are you okay with that?"

She grinned at him. Such an Idahoan dinner. The only thing that could make it more Idahoan was to add on a dessert like peach cobbler or apple pie. "I'd love it," she said. And she would. And she knew she shouldn't, but somehow, she couldn't seem to make herself care right at that exact moment. She would later.

Just not right then.

They went wandering up and down the aisles, arguing over the best salad dressing –

blue cheese was just downright nasty, obviously – and what to include in the salad. Not surprisingly, he didn't want tomatoes, not even little cherry tomatoes.

"Sometime, you're going to have to tell me what your major malfunction is about tomatoes," she said, dropping a small container into the cart for her own salad. He could leave them off his if he wanted. Far be it from her to force him to eat all the good stuff.

"Tomatoes are God's little joke on the world," he said as they browsed through the meat section, finally settling on a couple of marbled New York Strips. "They're food...with some assembly required." They'd moved over to the produce section, where he swung a 25-pound bag of russets into the cart. She didn't normally buy potatoes in those kinds of quantities, but considering how far south his potatoes would've gotten in the last two months, she figured he must be planning on taking the extras home with him when he left.

She cocked an eyebrow at him. "Some assembly required?"

"Yeah. Salsa, ketchup, spaghetti sauce – they're all great and wonderful. But you have to cook 'em up before you can eat them."

They moved towards the front checkout counters. "I guess that's one way of looking at it," she said. "But don't you at least love the smell of tomato plants during the summer? I always figured I'd throw in a few stems from a tomato plant into my bridal bouquet when I got married. I love that smell more than roses." She snapped her mouth shut. What on earth had possessed her to bring up marriage? She was such an idiot.

The cashier, a few years younger than her – was he Matthew Blank's younger brother? She wasn't quite sure – looked back and forth between them with interest. She sent him a pained smile. "How are you this evening?" she asked politely as Wyatt ran his debit card through the machine.

"Just fine, Officer Connelly," he said as he bagged their groceries up. She stifled a groan. Any chance that he had no idea who she was, was obviously out the window.

And the way he was looking between her and Wyatt? The chances of this little foray not getting back to her father were growing vanishingly smaller by the moment.

Whoops.

And yet, she couldn't seem to make herself care. She should. A tiny voice in the back of her mind was jumping up and down and screaming in panic right now but that part of her brain just seemed so far away. And unimportant.

Wyatt scooped up the grocery bags and a bag of dog food and asked, "Ready?"

"Yup." She turned away from the cash register, and the kid called out after her, "Have a good evening, Officer!"

She nodded, still heading for the door, trying to escape as quickly as possible.

What were the chances of her father not hearing about this? About zero percent or so.

Which, strangely, meant that she had nothing left to fear. If she was going to get into trouble for hobnobbing with Wyatt at the grocery store, well then, why not actually do something to get into trouble about? So far, she'd gone grocery shopping with a drop-dead sexy man...who smelled like garbage. Not exactly something to get arrested over.

Might as well make the crime worth the punishment.

CHAPTER 19

WYATT

E PUT ABBY'S GROCERIES into the backseat of her Toyota Corolla and then hopped in his truck to follow her to her house. Now that he thought about it, he wasn't quite sure where she lived. Surely not at home with her father, right? Because that would just about make for the most awkward dinner of his life.

Thankfully, she pulled up to the old Brightbart's place instead. He was surprised. He hadn't realized that the Brightbarts' children had sold it after Mr. Brightbart passed away last year.

"When did you buy this?" he asked as he helped her pack her groceries in, Maggie Mae settling down onto patio cushions on the front porch with a happy sigh.

"Oh, I haven't. Just renting," she said, unlocking her front door and flipping on the lights. Like a good police officer, she actually locked her house up when she left it. She was probably the only one in the county to do so.

"Really? The kids wanted to hang onto it after their dad died?" The Brightbart kids had scattered to the four winds after high school graduation. Wyatt was surprised they were the sentimental type.

"No, it just needs work done to it and they don't want to bother. There's some dirt-to-wood contact – the person who installed the back porch oughta be taken out back and shot – and the wiring isn't up to code." She shrugged. "It was easier for them to rent than to worry about it, and I get to have a whole house to myself, with no neighbors. It's kinda nice."

Just then, a gray-and-white tabby cat came

into the kitchen, butting her head up against Abby and then Wyatt's legs.

"Well, aren't you a pretty one?" he said, scooping her up into his arms. She rewarded him with a lick across his chin and a loud purr that rumbled through his chest.

"Jasmine," Abby said with a grin. "And she's a lover."

"I can tell," Wyatt murmured, running his hands over her head and down her back. "How does she like dogs?"

"Hates 'em. The only good dog is a dead dog." Abby flashed a smile at him. "She had more than a few cross words for me when I came home smelling like Maggie."

"She must've thought you'd turned traitor."

"Pretty much. I've never been given so many nasty looks in all my life."

Wyatt looked down at the purring cat in his arms, her eyes at half-mast as she enjoyed his attention.

"Hard to believe she could give someone a nasty look," he said, stroking through her soft fur. She had these little white paws that made her look like she had white gloves on. She had to be the prettiest cat he'd ever seen. And the nicest.

"Don't let her fool you," Abby said, arranging the food on the counter. "As much as she loves you right now? That's how much she hates dogs."

That was too damn bad. Wyatt set her down on the floor regretfully and with a mournful meow, Jasmine moved to the corner of the kitchen and began watching the preparations with crossed blue eyes. He turned back to Abby and smiled.

"Okay, now that I've broken your cat's heart by putting her down, what do you need me to do to help you get dinner ready?"

She set him to work chopping veggies for the salad – no nasty tomatoes, thank God – and they began chatting as they worked, about nothing in particular. It was so much damn fun to be around her. He wasn't sure if he'd ever enjoyed being around someone as much as he did her. He hadn't felt this at home around someone this quickly before, not even Shelly. It was casual and friendly and…

The sparks between them could very well set her crappy back porch on fire. She felt it too, he knew it. The heightened color on her cheeks. The sparkle in her eyes. The way she sent him sideways glances through her eyelashes, as if wanting to catch a peek of him without him noticing.

Of course he knew just what she was doing, because he was doing it too.

Being around Abby…it just lit him up inside. He hadn't felt this way around Shelly until a half-dozen dates in.

Stop it, Wyatt. You can't keep comparing Abby to Shelly. It isn't fair to either one of them.

He had to let her go – his dead wife. As much as it hurt, as much as the idea held little appeal to him, he knew that if he was ever going to be happy with someone else, he had to let her go. He had to let them both go – his daughter too.

It wasn't fair to keep comparing and letting ghosts get in the way of his future.

Abby carried plates over to the table. "Wanna grab the glasses?" she asked, jerking her head towards the cupboard. "They're in there."

He snagged a couple and a pitcher of juice she'd had him make after the salad was done. Once they carried everything to the table, it was quite the spread. They made a damn good pair in the kitchen.

He ducked his head towards her and then jerked himself short. He'd almost kissed her on the lips. It'd been instinctual – he'd always kissed Shelly on the lips before each meal. His parents had done it growing up, and so he'd picked up the habit once he got married. It just felt right.

But he couldn't lay one on his probation officer. No how, no way.

She caught the awkward movement and asked, "Are you okay?"

He sent her a pained grin. "Never better."

They began dishing up the food, and of

course, Wyatt had to give her shit about putting nasty-ass tomatoes onto her salad. She just rolled her eyes at him and popped one in her mouth, groaning with fake ecstasy. He couldn't help the laughter that bubbled up inside.

"So I should probably tell you why I hate them so much," he said, grinning at her.

She rolled her eyes. "No good reason, I'm sure of it."

"Say what you want, I think it's a damn good reason." He put a bite of his steak into his mouth and closed his eyes, chewing ecstatically. It wasn't a turkey sandwich, thank heavens. After months of eating that for lunch every day, he was quite sure he never wanted to see a turkey again in his life. Dead or alive. "My mom," he finally said, once he'd swallowed the steak.

"Your mom made you hate tomatoes?" Abby asked, one eyebrow cocked in disbelief.

"My mom was like all gardeners every-where – her seed catalog was bigger than her ability to can the stuff."

She giggled, a sound that he realized he

loved hearing. It was so much fun. He made a mental note to make her do it again. "Every year, my dad would go out and rototill this huge area – I swear, some years I think my father was trying to start a truck garden. And my mother was no better. She always encouraged him because this year, she was actually going to get everything picked and dried and frozen and canned on time. She never did, of course."

"Was your mom one of those people who went around and snuck zucchini into the backseats of cars?" Abby asked, laughing. The joke had always been that people in town only locked their car doors when zucchini season hit, so as to keep all of the unwanted squash out of their vehicles.

There was more than a little truth to that joke, which was of course why it was funny.

"Nope. That would require that she actually pick the zukes and deliver them somewhere. My mom rarely got to that point. She'd start out strong but once the heat of summer hit, she'd just wilt out in the sun. She didn't want to be out there, pulling weeds and watering, and us kids were always helping Dad with the farm chores. So she'd eventually just give up on it all and let it turn into a jungle of overgrown tomato plants, intermixed with the pumpkin vines that were sprawling out everywhere but never produced a damn thing."

"It's too cool up here for pumpkins," Abby said with a small laugh and shake of the head. "You can't grow a pumpkin up in the mountains."

"I know, but my mom was hopelessly optimistic. She kept trying every year; wanted to grow a pumpkin for Halloween. Never got one, not once."

"So how did all of that make you hate tomatoes?" Abby asked, a crease between her brow.

"Well, when fall hit and it was time to take care of the garden bed for the year, my dad was always too busy out in the fields, harvesting our wheat or oats or whatever it was that we were growing that year. My mom was just a little thing, and couldn't manhandle the rototiller – it weighed a ton – so as the oldest, it became my job to rototill everything under every fall. There I am, hot, sweaty, and smelling rotten tomatoes and zucchinis and green beans that were never picked, but I tell you what, the smell of rotten tomatoes is the worst smell of all. A fall or two of that would put anyone off their tomatoes."

Abby looked at him, grimacing, and then down at her plate. "Thanks. You don't think you could've told me that story when we were done eating?"

He shrugged unrepentantly. "At least now you know why I hate 'em."

"Anything else that your mom ruined you for life on?"

"Nope! Just rotten, black, stinking, mushy tomatoes."

She glared at him. "Now you're just trying to be a jackass."

"Totally possible." He sent her an innocent grin. "It's hard to imagine someone like me trying to be a jackass, but if I strain real hard, I guess I can see where you're coming from."

She bit her lip, trying to hold back her

laughter, and then it spilled out of her, a gorgeous cascade of sound. He settled back into his chair, content to hear that sound for the rest of his life.

And if that wasn't just the damndest thought he'd ever had.

CHAPTER 20

ABBY

*A*FTER ABBY PICKED the tomatoes off her salad and forced herself to eat every last one of them as if they were the most delicious thing she'd ever tasted, mock-glaring at Wyatt all the while, they began to chat about their childhoods. It was surprising to Abby to hear the similarities in their past; they had both lost their moms, and their dads…

Well, Abby got along better with her father than Wyatt had with his, but listening to him talk about his dad, there was still pride and love in his voice. They may've knocked heads over things, but there was still love there.

"Abby, I haven't ever told you about that night in the bar."

She shot him a wide-eyed look, surprised. She hadn't realized that he went out drinking, not after…

"No, not after Shelly and Sierra…not then," he said, reading her expression for exactly what it was. "Way back when your dad owned my place and lost it to the bank."

She nodded slowly, not sure what to say so she didn't say anything at all, just let him talk his piece.

"Well, it got around that I'd talked shit about your dad that night; that I told my buddies that I was going to show him how to run a farm." She nodded even more slowly this time. What could he possibly be driving at? That comment had deeply hurt her father's pride at a time when it was already in pieces. Losing a livelihood like that would destroy a smaller man than her father. Having the new owner spit in his face publicly just made it that much worse.

"I wasn't talking about him."

The silence dropped into the room, crushing everything else. She just stared at him, surprised, not able to really think through it. What he'd said. How was that…But everyone had said…

"I don't know who said it; I don't know how that got started. I was with two buddies from high school at the time, and they swear up, down, and sideways that it wasn't them. They know what I really said. Well—" He looked flustered. "I did say that, but I didn't mean your dad. That'd be just downright shitty, talking shit about a man who'd just lost his farm to the bank. No one needs that, not even your dad, and I think we all know we are never gonna be best buds."

She cracked a small smile at that, but it quickly faded. She just wanted to know the truth, after all this time.

"I was talking about my own dad. We butted heads big time – I just told you that. Now, years later, I think that it was because we were too much alike. My dad was kinda ornery, and I'm sure that you haven't noticed that character trait in me, but it's possible that others might have." She let out a belly laugh at that one and he grinned back in response, his first smile since he'd brought this topic up.

"We fought about everything, but mostly about those damn cows that Stetson brought back to the place. He'd talked my dad into it without even discussing it with me, and that farm was supposed to be mine. I'm the oldest, and..." He gulped. "Anyway, so there's my younger brother, mucking things up like he always did, bringing those cows onto the place; cows that had to be fed and watered and vaccinated and then they up and die on you without a moment's notice and they're dumber than a pile of rocks...

"I don't know of anyone who likes cows, not even cowboys. I'm a farmer – I like my wheat. It doesn't argue with me, break a leg in a hole, or escape through a pasture fence when you're not lookin'." She laughed again at that, but he was on a roll and she wasn't going to interrupt. This was something that had bothered him for a long time, and she was going to let him get it off his chest.

"So when I told my buddies that I was going to show 'him' how to run a place, I meant my dad. And yeah, I probably shouldn't have said that about my dad either, but it was long past time for me to move onto my own place when your dad's farm hit the...market." She was sure he was about to say "auction block," and she appreciated his thoughtfulness in choosing a more kind phrasing. "I was chafing, wanting to get out onto my own, and my relationship with my father was spiraling down, the more we butted heads. He always did spoil Stetson rotten. He came along as a surprise – did you know that?"

"I don't know that anyone ever came right out and said it, but based on the big age difference between him and Declan, I rather figured as much."

"Yeah, Mom and Dad thought they were done – they had Dec and I and things were great. And then along came this squalling little baby, and he was truly the baby of the family, in more ways than one. He got whatever he wanted, and in the end, that meant he got the Miller Family Farm too. Over 130 years in the Miller family, and my dad up and wills the damn thing to Stetson. And then the dumbass almost loses it to the bank. I don't know what I would've done if Jennifer hadn't come along and helped him save it."

Abby nodded. That had been the gossip of the town for months – first, that Stetson had gotten so far behind on his payments that he almost lost the family farm, and then that Jennifer, an outsider and from a bank, no less, had been the one to figure out what to do to save it.

She guessed that Stetson didn't mind in the end, since he'd married her and they were expecting a baby this spring but she could see how Wyatt might not take that as a consolation. A family didn't hold onto a farm for over a hundred years and then not care if they lost it to foreclosure.

Her dad could attest to that one.

"I appreciate the information, Wyatt," she said softly, stroking his hand resting on the table. She probably shouldn't be touching him; she probably shouldn't be having this meal with him, but right then, all of the "probablies" in the world didn't matter. "That makes a lot of sense. Have you tried to talk to my dad about it?"

"Oh yeah. Once. He didn't want to hear me out. He walked away and…well, I'm not the kind of man who will try twice. If you're going to spit on my attempt to reach out to you, I don't have much use for ya."

She nodded. It was true; he'd swallowed his pride to even try once. She wasn't surprised to hear that her father wouldn't listen. He wasn't the kind of guy to listen much, ever, but certainly not to someone he hated.

"Well, I appreciate you telling me, really. That means a lot to me."

She was surprised by just how much it did mean to her, actually. She thought she'd let that go a long time ago, but hearing the reasoning and knowing that Wyatt hadn't intended to be a jackass that night…

It was nice to hear.

He smiled at her then, and it wasn't one of his teasing grins or snarky grins or…

It was a sexy grin. A heart-stopping grin. A panty-melting grin.

The butterflies took up twerking again and this time, she couldn't even manage to dredge up the willpower to tell them to stop. Or even want them to stop. Wyatt, looking at her like she was dessert?

She swallowed hard and his eyes darkened more. The world stopped − she stopped, he stopped, they just stared at each other and she felt herself drifting towards him, infinitesimally closer, and−

"Meow!" Jasmine said, wrapping herself around Abby's leg. She jerked back and stared down at Jasmine in shock. Jasmine looked back up at her, huge crossed blue eyes clearly begging for a plate to clean.

"Oh Lordy, child," Abby said with a groan. She looked back at Wyatt but the mood was broken. He was standing up from the table, carrying his plate to the sink. Abby normally let Jasmine lick her plate clean every night, but tonight? Nope. If Abby wasn't going to get any action, then neither was Jasmine.

It was the first time that Abby had ill thoughts towards her cat since the night Jasmine had jumped down from the windowsill above her bed and landed right on her face, her back paw digging into her eye socket. She had more than a few choice words for Jasmine that night, too.

Abby stood up from the table and together, in a silence only growing more awkward the longer it lingered, they cleared off the table and loaded the ancient olive green dishwasher. Finally finished and still not a word had passed between them. Abby wiped her hands on her jeans, her mouth dry.

"Well, goodnight!" she said, overly cheerful and loud and oh heavens, she sounded like an idiot and she knew it.

"Goodnight," Wyatt said, sticking out his hand to shake just as she went in for a hug, so they did this awkward-as-could-be hug/handshake combo that probably looked as ridiculous as it felt. He pulled back and said, "I'll let myself out," and then he was gone, out the door and into the winter night.

She shut the door behind him and slumped against it. Then slowly, methodically, she whacked her head backwards, once, twice, three times.

"Abby Connelly, you are a first-class idiot."

Jasmine sat down in front of her, looking at her quizzically. "Meowww…"

Abby sent her a death glare. "And you, young lady! No plates from the dinner table for…for a week!" She felt ridiculous threatening her cat that way, but then again, wasn't that just this whole evening rolled up into one word? Ridiculous?

Who invited their prisoner over for dinner? And laughed with him? And made googly eyes at him?

Not a county police officer, that's for damn sure.

She was an idiot, through and through.

With a sigh, she climbed the stairs to her bedroom. "C'mon, Jasmine," she said wearily.

"Let's go to bed. Things can only be better in the morning, right?"

But as she settled down into bed after changing into her PJs and brushing her teeth, she stared at the ceiling and wondered if that was true after all. What, exactly, was going to be better in the morning? Wyatt was still going to be on probation and her father was still going to hate him and she still couldn't be attracted to him.

No doubt about it, her endlessly positive outlook on life was starting to garner a little tarnish to its shine.

And she wasn't quite sure what to think about that.

CHAPTER 21

WYATT

*I*T WAS THE COLD that woke him up.

He was shivering uncontrollably and his nose…he pulled his hand up and out of the sleeping bag to poke at it, shivering even harder when the winter air burrowed through his layers of sweaters and winter coat to steal up his arm. His nose didn't fall off when he wiggled it, though, which he took as a good sign.

With a groan, he opened his eyes, staring up at the bead board ceiling of his three-season porch. Yup, it was definitely the fourth season of the year. At the moment, it was hard for him to remember just how he could think that sleeping outside in January was better than sleeping in a house that smelled like rotten garbage. His frozen, aching limbs told him otherwise.

Of course, as frozen as his nose was, he might not be able to smell anything any longer, a real positive in his book.

He swung his legs over the edge of the patio loveseat, which had been much too short for him to stretch out on, which had just added to the night's misery. He unzipped the sleeping bag and forced his legs to carry him into the house, where he breathed in the warm air.

Warm, disgusting, stinking air.

He started hacking, trying to expel the taste and smell from his lungs and throat.

Well, there went that theory – even after a night outside, his nose still worked well enough for him to smell. Which was probably good in the grand scheme of things, but not really that appreciated at the moment.

He unplugged his phone from the wall outlet and walked to the other end of the house, as far away from the kitchen as he could get. He turned his phone on and was pleasantly surprised to see it light up. He wasn't sure if seven weeks of disuse would've killed the battery or not. Some good news this morning, anyway.

He debated, and finally called Adam first. He needed to swallow his pride and get it over with.

The asking-for-a-favor part.

It went against everything in him, but he could do it. Mostly because he had to.

"Hey Wyatt!" Adam's voice, lit up and happy, rang in his ear. "I didn't know you got out!"

"Just yesterday," Wyatt said, the ball of nerves growing tighter. Here it was. Here was the big ask. He could do it.

Because he had to.

"Listen, I have a…" He tried to say "favor" but couldn't get it past his throat. "Question to ask," he finished. "I was assigned 75 community service hours from the Ada judge. Can I serve them at your place?" The last part came out in a rush, but at least it did come out. He hoped Adam had heard the question and wouldn't make him repeat it. It was bad enough the first time.

"My place?" Adam echoed, confused. Wyatt knew from his tone of voice that he was imagining that Wyatt wanted to come over and do his dishes or something. Oh hell no. Wyatt hated doing his own dishes; he wasn't about to spend 75 hours doing someone else's.

"At your therapy camp. With the kids and the horses," he clarified. And not a dish in sight. At least, he hoped there were no dirty dishes in the riding arena.

"Oh, right, of course! I'd love that. Oh Wyatt, just wait until you meet these kids. They're incredible. So much love in them – you've never met a better bunch of children in your life."

Sierra's face flashed before Wyatt's eyes, smiling and bright. The pain and love tore at him equally. She would've been seven in May. He missed her so damn much. Maybe being around other children would…help.

Either help or kill him straight off. One or the other.

It was a tough pill to swallow, the idea of moving on past Sierra's death. A part of him felt like if he let it go, then it didn't count. It didn't matter after all. But…

Maybe he could see other children her age and teach them what he knew. There were only a few men in the county who were better with horses than him. And he liked kids okay. As long as they weren't screaming or throwing up, he'd be fine.

"That'd be great, Adam," Wyatt got out, his stomach still a ball of nerves. "What time do you want me there?"

"Around 2:30 – would that work? That way, we can go over some things before the kids get here after school."

"Sounds great. See you then." They hung up, and Wyatt stared at his phone for a moment.

That hadn't actually killed him.

A smile crept across his face, growing by the moment. Damn, and wasn't that just a great feeling? He'd asked for a favor, and Adam had said yes. He hadn't ridiculed him for needing help or anything.

Before his grin could get ridiculously out of control, he pulled out the phone book for the Long Valley area from his desk in the den, batting away the dust that came with it. A couple of sneezes later, and he'd found a cleaning company in Franklin.

When he explained that he'd been "gone" from his home for two months and that he needed a cleaning crew out to his place on an emergency basis, the older, placid-sounding woman assured him that they could be there by that afternoon. He thanked her and hung up.

Now, it was time to find something to do that was far, far away from his house.

Jorge.

Duh.

His farm manager was his only year-round full-time employee, and because of the state of his house when he got home last night, he hadn't thought to go out and even tell him that he'd been released. Now was as good a time as any.

He stepped outside and took a deep breath of the bracing, freezing air, blessedly free of smells. It was terrific, it really was, to be back home.

He took off at a brisk walk down the snow-encrusted dirt lane towards the double-wide trailer that served as Jorge's home. Maggie was by his side, her nose and tail going a mile a minute. "You're damn happy to be home too, aren't ya, girl?" Wyatt said with a smile. She grinned up at him for just a moment, he'd swear it was true, and then her nose was back to the ground and she was sniffing again.

Yeah, it was damn nice to be home again.

Just as he got to the front porch of the double-wide, the snow crunching under foot as he went, Jorge opened up the front door and stepped outside. His weathered face lit up when he caught sight of Wyatt. "¡*Hola, señor!*" he said. "You *casa!*"

They tended to talk a mixture of Spanglish to each other, punctuated when necessary with hand gestures. It was a cross between charades and high school Spanish. It kept Wyatt from forgetting too much from his high school days, anyway.

"*Hola*," he said warmly, shaking Jorge's hand. "*¿Cómo estás?*"

"*Bien, bien.* Come. My chickens! *Huevos*, for you." He gestured and they walked into the cramped double-wide together. Jorge chattered quickly to his wife, Maria, in Spanish, as grandkids came crowding into the living room. Wyatt greeted them and chatted with them for a minute; unlike their grandparents, the kids were completely fluent in both Spanish and English, which meant that at times, they acted as translators between Wyatt and Jorge.

Wyatt knew that some of the ranchers in the valley wouldn't put up with the language barrier and would've fired Jorge long ago, but he was a damn hard worker, and he also had a large family to support. Wyatt couldn't imagine chucking him out into the snow, no matter how many games of charades he had to play.

Jorge pulled a dozen eggs out of the fridge.

"For you, for you," he said, shoving the carton into Wyatt's hands. "*Bienvenido a casa.* Happy to see you."

Shooting Jorge a grin, he flipped the carton lid open to admire the double row of brown and white eggs. "*Gracias,*" he said. "*Muchas gracias.*" He knew how precious eggs were during the winter; mid-January was probably the slowest time of the year for egg laying, and he knew Jorge's family could use the eggs.

But he also knew that Jorge took pride in giving them to him, and if there was one thing that Wyatt Miller understood, it was pride.

After some high fives with the grandkids, he made his way back outside into the bitter cold. He hurried to drop off the carton back at his house and then took to walking the fields, checking fences and reacquainting himself with his farm. Afterwards, he'd make a trip over to his barn to curry and feed his horses.

Yeah, it felt damn good to be back home.

CHAPTER 22

ABBY

*A*BBY WALKED DOWN the jail cell block to get to the supply room in the back. She needed to put replacement batteries in all of the smoke detectors every other month, per county law, and so they kept a huge tub of them in the back supply closet.

As she passed Wyatt's cell, her heart hurt a little. It was stupid. She was so happy for him; so glad that he'd gotten out and was a free man, relatively speaking. Sure, he had to put in his community service hours, which thankfully Vet Whitaker had agreed to be the sponsor for, but that and some counseling were light years ahead of being locked up behind bars.

So she was happy for Wyatt, she really was. It was a good thing, having him out and free again and moving on with his life.

She began pulling batteries out of the tub, counting mechanically as her brain spun through what was *really* bothering her: She missed him.

She should be glad for him that he was finally free again. That Maggie Mae was able to run in the fields again. And she was, she really was.

But a selfish part of her wanted him back in jail. His cell was so empty every time she walked past it. And it would always be "Wyatt's cell" to her. He'd become such a part of her day; teasing her or simply reading quietly as she walked past, but he'd been there, always there.

No, that wasn't right. She didn't want him back in jail again. She wanted him out and free. She wanted him happy. She just…wanted to be with him too.

She scooped the batteries up and carried them back up to the front of the jail. It was time to pull out the ladder and begin replacing batteries. Oh, the glamorous life of a small-town cop. When she went to the Cleveland Elementary School on Career Day and talked about being a cop, she always somehow managed to leave out any mention of changing batteries in smoke detectors.

Finally, Morland came in and relieved her so she could head home. With a happy sigh, she headed to her house and began...

Slowly driving herself insane. She tried watching TV but quickly flicked it off. Nothing on there appealed to her. She pulled out her favorite author's new book, *The Girl with the Make-Believe Husband*, but then all she could think about was husbands and marrying and...

She stood up. She'd make herself a cup of tea. It was too late for coffee; with the caffeine jitters, she'd never be able to go to sleep. She'd just brew up some Earl Gray and sip it while... knitting. She could knit. Or rather, she'd knitted in the past. No time like the present to reacquaint herself with her knitting needles. Maybe she could knit some scarves for the homeless shelter in Boise. That'd be a good thing to do. They always needed—

Her personal cell phone rang, and Abby practically leapt for it. Anything to do that wasn't thinking about Wyatt Miller was a Very Good Thing at that point.

"Hello?" she said breathlessly, shoving the phone between her ear and shoulder as she put her tea kettle under the faucet.

"Hi, Abby?" Wyatt's voice rumbled through the phone, warm and friendly. She almost dropped the phone into the overflowing water but just managed to catch it and shove it back between her shoulder and ear before flipping the gushing water off. She sank against the edge of the sink.

"How did you get my personal number?" she asked, totally confused. She hadn't given it to him; she never gave it out to prisoners. Not that she would've told him no if he'd asked for it, because he was Wyatt Miller, not just any ol' prisoner, but he hadn't asked, and thus she hadn't given it to him.

"It's a small town, Abby. It's not hard to get someone's number if you want to."

She rolled her eyes and then realized that he couldn't see her. *Gah.* Sometimes, small towns were a little too up-in-her-space for her.

Of course, it wasn't that she was upset that he was calling. It'd just thrown her off, was all. She poured some of the extra water down the drain and then put the kettle on the stove. "What can I do for you, Mr. Miller?"

Which was a ridiculous thing to call him, considering everything, but it just sort of slipped out. She had a sinking feeling in her stomach that she was going to screw this relationship up out of sheer ineptitude, just like she had every other relationship she'd attempted over the years.

She was 33 and single for a reason, and she couldn't blame all of it on the fact that her father was the sheriff, or her weight.

He hesitated for a moment and she was sure she'd completely blown it, but he finally went on and she blew out a breath of relief. "I've really been enjoying working with the kids and Adam this past week," he said. "I started to wonder if you'd like to come along with me? I know how much you like horses."

That was true. Pretty much everyone knew how much she liked horses; it didn't take much to know that. You just had to know her back in her high school days, when she was on the Long Valley Roping Team and was winning most calf roping events that she entered. Her favorite horse of all time, Black Diamond, was the only thing that got her through her mother's death.

Horses were expensive, though, and she hadn't been able to afford the upkeep in the last couple of years. Her heart yearned for it. "Yes, please," she said, and she was a little embarrassed by how breathlessly happy she sounded, but she couldn't help herself. He might as well have asked her if she wanted a pot of gold delivered to her house in the morning.

Except time with horses was more priceless than gold.

"Fine, fine. I'll come by your house tomorrow around three – will you be home?"

"Yeah, I work the morning shift tomorrow, so I'll be cutting it close, but I'll be here."

"See you then." He hung up without another word, which was just when her tea kettle let out an ear-piercing whistle. The water was hot. She pulled it off the burner and flipped open the cap at the end of the spout to stop the whistling. She just stood there and stared at it though, not moving another inch.

He wanted her to spend time with the horses. He was going to come over and pick her up.

Was this some sort of…date?

A small smile that grew larger the more she thought, burst into place. Wyatt Miller was asking her out on a date, but he was so out of touch, his "date" was asking his parole officer to come do his community service with him.

She was pretty sure this had to be a first. She

probably shouldn't laugh, but it was so damn typical of Wyatt. She wasn't sure who else she knew would think that community service was a romantic atmosphere, but at the same time…

She couldn't find it in herself to be disappointed in the lack of romance in their upcoming date. Any date of any kind with Wyatt was one to be excited about.

But also, she could sorta-kinda-maybe pass this off as not-a-date if word somehow got back to her father. She could simply be checking up on him. Making sure everything was going okay. Sure, she'd never heard of a parole officer doing that before, but why not? They were a small town and made up rules as they went along all the time. This could just be another made-up rule.

She sat down on the couch with her cup of tea but realized that she was now struggling with another problem: She was filled with a completely different set of jitters. Before, she hadn't been able to settle on anything because she missed Wyatt. Now, she could hardly remember to blow on her tea before sipping it because she was going to see Wyatt. She wasn't sure which state of mind was worse for her.

Jasmine jumped up and cuddled next to her, stretching her paw out across Abby's lap as she stroked down the soft fur.

"Jasmine, I need to get my head on straight." Jasmine's purr rumbled through her leg, which Abby decided to take as agreement.

"Even though Wyatt isn't my prisoner anymore, he is still on parole. Then even after he gets off that, the idea that I could date him is… ludicrous. Simply nuts. Father would have a heart attack, and then rise up off the table at the ER and strangle me with his bare hands."

Jasmine kept purring. Abby put down her empty tea cup on the end table, and then began petting Jasmine with both hands. The volume on her cat increased exponentially.

"So tomorrow afternoon is going to be nothing more than a parole officer checking up on someone and making sure they're not drinking or doing drugs or beating someone up." Truth be told, she hadn't heard of Wyatt touching a drop of alcohol since the night his family had been killed by that drunk driver, and she'd be willing to bet next year's salary on the fact that he'd never taken drugs.

And if he was going around beating people up, the sheriff's department would be the first ones to hear about it.

Which meant that if they were going to get all technical about it, there was…well, zero reason for her to go with him out to Adam's place.

Other than she just wanted to.

Dammit.

She scooped Jasmine up in her arms and flicked off the living room light. "Let's go to bed," she said, cuddling Jasmine to her as she navigated through the darkened living room. "I have a non-date date to go on tomorrow, and something tells me I'll need all the rest I can get to make it through it."

Jasmine gave her a quick swipe across the lips with her roughened pink tongue, which Abby promptly decided to assign absolutely no meaning to at all.

CHAPTER 23

WYATT

HE PULLED UP in front of the old Brightbart's place – Abby's place; he'd need to start calling it that, no matter what habit dictated – and sat for just a moment in his truck, staring out through his windshield. He hadn't slept well the night before, so nervous about this whole date – was it a date? – that he'd just tossed and turned the whole night through. He'd spent the morning trying to keep himself busy so he wouldn't totally make himself crazy as he waited for three o'clock to arrive, but he'd be the first one to admit that he was failing.

He left his truck rumbling – it was hard on diesels to be turned off and on in the cold – and headed up to the front door. Now wasn't the time for nerves. He was just picking Abby up and they were going to head over and hang out with a bunch of kids who loved horses and he wasn't going to kiss Abby and everything was going to be fine.

Just fine.

He raised his hand to knock on the door but it swung open from underneath his knuckles to reveal Abby, smiling and heading out the door. "Ready?" she said as she went past him.

He spun around and stared at her as she hurried up her walk towards his truck. Why had she been lying in wait like that? And why was she in such a hurry?

He went after her, held her door open for her, and then went around to the driver's side and swung in. Pulling out and heading out into the countryside towards Adam's place, he cast about for something to ask, finally barking out, "How'd you sleep?"

Except he winced as the words came out because they seemed rather…aggressive. He sounded like he was demanding, not asking. She smelled so good – the lemon scent wafting off her – and looked so good in a pair of form-fitting Wranglers and pearl-snap shirt, that he was lucky he was keeping his truck on the road. He was having a real hard time facing forward, to be honest. He was all mixed up inside, and nervous as hell.

He gripped the steering wheel harder, trying to convince himself that breathing was a good idea.

"I slept fine," she said, sending him a sideways glance. He was aware of every move she made, like it was being telegraphed directly to his brain and when her tongue flicked out and wet her lips, he felt it real strongly…somewhere else.

He shifted in his seat.

"Good," he grunted.

"How's your week out there been going so far?" Abby asked.

"Fine, fine," he said. "The kids in this program are...good."

He stumbled for a moment. That wasn't strictly true in the well-behaved sense. They often tested boundaries and he had to keep a close eye on them. But they were sure awesome to be around. He'd found himself falling in love with a couple of them, especially Juan. He was a foster kid, only nine and wanting nothing more than to be loved...and being so scared no one would.

He saw a lot of himself in Juan.

He cleared his throat again and grumped out, "You'll like the kids. And the horses."

Why was he being like this? The other night at her house, he hadn't acted this way.

Maybe because he hadn't spent the twenty-four hours previous to that night staring at the ceiling, working himself up into knots. Maybe he shouldn't ever see Abby except as a surprise. He could only accidentally run her down with his cart at the Shop 'N Go before being allowed to spend time with her. Then he wouldn't have time to work himself up into a lather beforehand.

Seemed like a good enough plan, minus the randomness of it all. He wanted to see Abby a lot, not just occasionally.

He swallowed hard. It was thoughts like that that had him wrapped up in knots.

"I appreciate the invitation," she said with a gentle smile, turning in her seat to look at him. "I have a couple of friends who have horses and let me come over and ride them sometimes, but I sure do miss it."

"Why don't you have horses out at the Brightbart's place? They have that barn − I'm sure you could house a horse in there and put it out to pasture during the summer."

She shrugged. "I'm sure you know this, but horses are…expensive, and then the Brightbart kids − they want to be able to rent out the pasture as another source of income. So if I want a horse, I have to pay extra for that pasture, on top of vet care, hay, and everything else that a horse needs. Plus, no horse should be alone, so I really ought to have two, which just about doubles all the costs…" She heaved a sigh. "It's a lot for a deputy's salary, you know?"

He did know. Money was always tight — that's just the way the world was. If he spent a little more on one thing, that meant cutting back elsewhere. Truth was, being locked up in jail at the tail-end of harvest this past year could've ruined him financially, and he knew it, and the judge knew it. He was damn lucky that he had Declan in his corner, or the bank could've ended up with his place back on the auction block for someone else to take a chance on.

They pulled into Adam's place, which was actually his mom's place. Ruby had arthritis and wasn't able to live by herself anymore. He'd moved back in with her to help take care of her years ago.

Adam was good people.

Wyatt shot Abby a smile. "Ready?" he asked, a little less gruffly than before. He felt a tiny bit more at ease than previously, and he realized it was because she'd opened up to him about finances. That wasn't the kind of topic you talked about with just anyone, and yet, she'd trusted him enough to tell him the truth.

That meant a lot.

She grinned back at him. "Ready!"

They hopped out of the truck and towards the barn. It was horse time, and Wyatt couldn't wait.

CHAPTER 24

ABBY

WHEN SHE'D RILED herself up last night about going out with Wyatt on their non-date date, she'd imagined a lot of scenarios playing out in her head, anywhere from just hanging out as friends to him sweeping her off her feet and finding a hayloft to make love to her in. Granted, that was a far-fetched one but it was her daydreams, dammit, and thus in them, she could make love to Wyatt without her father going into nuclear meltdown over it.

The one scenario she hadn't imagined? A morose Wyatt barking at her.

At first, she couldn't fathom what was going on. He'd been so totally different the night they ate dinner together, and that had just been a week ago. He'd obviously wanted to be around her, because he asked her to come with him today. So why was he snapping at her like a wounded animal?

But the more they talked in the truck, the more she noticed small things about him – the light sheen of sweat on his forehead, despite the freezing temperatures outside. The way his hands were gripping the steering wheel like it was the only thing keeping him from going completely insane.

And then she had an epiphany – Wyatt was nervous. Wyatt Miller, the King of Swagger. The no-bullshit-from-anyone man. He was nervous to talk to *her*.

It was that adorable nervousness wrapped up in a shield of pride that made her open up to him about finances. She didn't go around blabbing about money to just anyone; she wasn't even sure she talked much about it with Chloe. But she had a feeling that if she just opened herself up a little, if she just made herself vulnerable to Wyatt in a small way, that he'd lower his defenses, too.

She didn't say that she totally understood him yet, but when they arrived at Adam's place and hopped out, the smile he sent her was friendly…and heart-stopping.

Of course, just being around Wyatt was bad for the heart. She wouldn't be surprised if the doctor put her on arrhythmia medication at the rate she was going.

Adam came hurrying over, a big smile splitting his face. "Wyatt, you old dog, you! You didn't tell me you were going to be bringing a good lookin' helper with you today. How did you manage to con someone like Abby to come here with you?" Adam and Wyatt shook hands and then Adam gave her a hug and peck on the cheek.

"She started looking sickly and I realized that she hadn't spent much time around horses lately. I figured we'd better inoculate her with some horse time real soon or she was bound to keel over on us."

Abby stuck her tongue out at him playfully, but inside, she was surprised to hear him joke around like this. Was this what he was like around his friends? The only other person she'd ever seen him truly relax around was Declan.

Which, come to think of it, Adam and Declan were his two closest friends, so that stood to reason.

She filed that tidbit of info away for future reference.

"Well, c'mon then!" Adam said, turning and heading towards the indoor riding arena. "The kids just got here and are probably scaling the walls without me there to watch 'em."

They headed towards the arena, the open door letting a stream of pale light out onto the ground in the weak wintry afternoon. The sun was lost behind an overcast sky, and Abby wouldn't be surprised if it didn't make an appearance for another week, or even month. Long Valley wasn't the place for people with Seasonal Affective Disorder, that was for sure.

As they walked into the arena, Abby watched Adam's hips move in that loose-limbed way that every cowboy seemed to have. How was it that she wasn't attracted to Adam? He was handsome, established, and a real sweetie. She should be madly in love with him.

Of course, he was madly in love with Chloe, even if Chloe couldn't see it, and that definitely put a damper on things. But since when had her heart only done the logical thing?

No, if it was going to make logical choices, Wyatt wouldn't be anywhere on the list.

And yet…

"Hey everyone, come gather 'round!" Adam called out. The kids, who had been climbing on every horizontal and vertical surface in the building, came tumbling over. There were only about ten of them – maybe fifteen? She couldn't tell because they seemed to be vibrating with energy, making it hard to keep track of them – but as a whole…they were quite the group. She could see why Adam would appreciate some extra hands on board.

Once everyone was quieted and mostly looking their direction, Adam said, "Ms. Connelly—"

"Abby," she said, interrupting him. She got called Deputy Connelly enough at work. She didn't need to add formality here too.

"Abby is going to be helping us out today. Can you say, 'Hi, Abby'?"

"Hi, Abby!" the chorus of voices rang out.

"Awesome. Now, remember what we talked about yesterday when it comes to brushing a horse. Do you brush from its head to its tail, or from its tail to its head?" He demonstrated the question over a fine-looking roan who was standing nearby. She noticed that when he went backwards, he didn't actually touch the horse but instead brushed the air just above. Thoughtful to the very last.

"Head to tail!" The group was nothing if not enthusiastic.

"Good job. All right, go find your brushes or curries. Always let the horse smell you before you start brushing them, and only one child per horse!"

The kids scattered, grabbing brushes and curries before hurrying to their favorite horses. Abby decided to just wander around and keep her eye on the kids to see if anyone needed some guidance.

After settling a squabble between two kids who wanted the same horse, she found herself drawn to an adorable little girl with hair in long brown braids. She squinted up at Abby through her coke-bottle glasses and then broke out into a grin that revealed a mouth full of metal. They were obviously in the middle of fixing her teeth. She had Down Syndrome, but as soon as she opened her mouth, Abby could tell she wasn't letting that hold her back.

"Hi Abby, I'm Genny. With a G. This is Sonny. Want to help brush him?"

"Sure," Abby said, accepting the soft brush thrust into her hands. She stood off to the side of Sonny so he could get a good look at her, and then put her hand out for him to sniff. He snuffled against the palm of her hand, obviously hoping for a treat. She laughed and ran her hand down his neck. "I don't have anything for you right now, you big beggar," she said. "Maybe later."

She turned to Genny with a G. "Remind me how to brush Sonny again?"

She wanted to see Genny's technique, but the question worked just how she'd wanted it to. Genny's face lit up at the importance of showing a grown-up how to do something.

"You have to start here," she said, snagging the brush from Abby and positioning it over Sonny's neck, "and brush him down to here." She dragged her arm all the way across Sonny's body until she got to the hindquarters.

"You're pretty good at this," Abby said to her with a smile. "What happens if you try to brush here?" she asked, indicating the belly of the horse.

"It tickles them!" Genny said, nodding to emphasize. Just then, Wyatt came around the corner with a small bucket of oats.

"Oh, and we get to feed them oats every day!" Genny said, squealing and grabbing the bucket from Wyatt.

"What do you say to Wyatt?" Abby asked.

"Thank you, Wyatt," Genny said sincerely, then spun back towards Sonny. She dipped her hand into the bucket and pulled out a huge handful of oats, letting Sonny snuffle and suck the oats right out of her hand like a vacuum cleaner on high. Abby hid her grin behind her hand. There was nothing more fun than feeding a horse some oats, except maybe watching the cutest little girl she ever did see feed a horse some oats.

Wyatt was still standing next to her, and she turned and grinned up at him. He grinned back and her damn heart did that irregular rhythm thing again. She gulped hard. If she was going to guard her heart against Wyatt Miller, she needed to start by not wanting to be around him.

She wasn't entirely sure that was possible.

After another couple of hours of working with the kids on how to bridle a horse and lead them around the arena, eventually the parents and foster parents began arriving to pick up their kids. Genny threw her arms around Abby when her mother came walking up. "Are you going to come back again, Abby? Please oh please oh please?"

Her mother, an older woman with a permanently tired look on her face, reached out for Genny's arm. "Now don't go bothering this nice lady—"

"It's okay," Abby said, breaking in gently. She knelt down in front of Genny so they could give each other a proper hug. "I will definitely be back," she whispered into Genny's ear. "Thanks for showing me how to brush a horse."

Genny smacked a kiss loudly on her cheek. "I'm the best at brushing," she announced, and then, grabbing her mom's hand, they walked towards the front door. Her mom was busy trying to get Genny into her winter coat, while Genny was just as busy telling her mom about every horse in the arena, punctuating the comments with hand gestures. It looked a bit like the mom was trying to wrestle a calf into submission, which probably accounted for the permanently tired look on her face.

Abby shot Wyatt a grin and he smiled back.

"You sure are good with kids," he said, as they made their way towards the arena doors.

Abby shrugged. "They're easy to get to know. They all want to be your friend, and they all think you're cool because you're an adult. It isn't until they hit their teenage years that they become impossible."

Wyatt threw his head back and laughed. "That's about the long and short of it," he agreed dryly.

After saying goodbye to Adam, they climbed into Wyatt's truck to head back home. She stared out the passenger side window, a stab of pain running through her.

Yeah, she loved kids, a whole lot. But unfortunately, that didn't mean a damn thing.

Just like loving Wyatt would never go anywhere.

CHAPTER 25

WYATT

THEY ARRIVED AT ABBY'S HOUSE. Always the gentleman, Wyatt hurried around to open the truck door for her. She slipped out past him smelling of lemon, but also of horses and oats and the great outdoors. He'd thought she'd smelled good before, but now…

"Are you wanting to come back with me tomorrow?" he asked as they made their way up the frozen path towards her house.

"I would, but I don't get off until four to-morrow. Is that too late, you think?" She looked up at him questioningly, biting her lower lip.

She'd unlocked her front door but hadn't opened it yet. He couldn't quite make out the expression on her face because their breaths were making clouds in the frosty air, blocking his view.

That's the reason that he gave for leaning forward towards her. Just so he could see her face a little better. Nothing more.

"If we only get you for an hour or two, it's totally worth it," he said softly. "I think Adam will be happy to have you for however long you can be there."

Which was probably true, but they both knew that Adam wasn't who he was thinking about just then. He wanted nothing more than to lean forward and nibble on that lower lip that she currently had snagged between her teeth. He wanted to bury his hands in her hair and kiss her until she couldn't speak.

He wanted...her.

"Okay," she whispered softly. He was just inches from her. She gulped hard and then felt for the doorknob behind her back. "I must go now. Goodbye," and then she was twisting the knob and practically falling into the house, shutting the door behind her with a whispered *click* that sounded like a cannon in the cold winter air.

Wyatt jerked back and stared at the door. He had to get himself under control. It was ridiculous for him to crave someone like he craved Abby, if she didn't feel the same way about him.

The thing was, he couldn't quite convince himself that she didn't feel that same way about him. She was a mess of contradictions, and was confusing the ever-livin' hell outta him.

He headed back to his truck and threw it into gear. He needed to go for a long, punishing ride on Elvis. Get his head screwed on straight. Get a deep breath back into his lungs.

Get Deputy Abby Connelly out of his system.

CHAPTER 26

ABBY

TODAY WAS GOING to be a good day.

Today was going to be an *awesome* day. She was going to have fun with the kids and she was going to spend some quality time around horses and she was absolutely, positively not going to flirt with Wyatt. Or stare at him. Or let her heart get all weird around him.

She just wasn't going to allow it.

And that was final.

She quickly changed out of her deputy uniform and then headed over to Adam's place. They'd already be in gear and working because she was so late getting there, but it'd be fun to go anyway. She turned up the country western music on the radio and sang at the top of her lungs on the drive over, trying to give herself something else to do that didn't involve thinking about Wyatt.

Because she totally wasn't going to think about Wyatt today.

She parked off to the side and walked into the arena, the bright lights a wonderful, warm welcome.

A couple of the kids came running over to say hello, including Genny, but Abby couldn't help searching Wyatt out. It didn't seem like she was really "there" until she'd made eye contact with him. Which totally went against her resolutions made just five minutes before.

A contradiction she was totally going to ignore.

He caught her eye and smiled. As she walked with the chattering kids over to the horse Wyatt was working with, she only listened with half an ear to the updates since yesterday. They'd been allowed to put a saddle blanket on the horses today, and this was apparently the highlight of everyone's life thus far. As one kid, Juan, said, "Those things are heavy! Wyatt only had to help me a little, though."

Wyatt winked at him. "Well, when you get as tall as me, you're not gonna need anyone's help then."

Juan nodded seriously at his words, and Abby bit back her smile. She could tell Juan had a lot of pride. A lot like someone else she knew.

Wyatt sent her a knowing smile and winked at her, too. She felt a flush work its way through her body and tried to stifle her groan. She couldn't.

Couldn't.

Couldn't.

Couldn't.

As the kids scattered, heading back to their horses, Wyatt and Juan began discussing when to use a soft brush versus a metal-toothed curry, and Genny slipped her hand into Abby's. "Wanna see Sonny? I haven't fed him any oats yet today because no one would give them to me."

Translation: *I want you to give me oats so I can feed Sonny.*

Abby laughed. Wyatt wasn't the only one to have a mini-me in the group. "Oh, we better make sure he gets a little," she said, patting Genny on the shoulder.

Genny grinned up at her and then asked, "But why can't we just feed the horses lots and lots of oats? Why can we only feed 'em a little?"

"Well, oats are good for a horse, but only in moderation. Hold on, let me get you a bucket." She'd watched Wyatt the day before, and knew where to get the small buckets and oats from. She filled one up and brought it back to Genny who was waiting as patiently as her little body would let her.

Genny grabbed at the bucket, and Abby said quietly, "What do you say, Genny?"

She paused for a moment, scrunching up her nose. "Thank you, Abby."

With a smile, Abby let go of the bucket and Genny bounced over to Sonny, shoving a fistful of oats into his muzzle.

"Think about it like this," Abby said, returning to the oats discussion for a moment. "Apples are good for you, right?"

"Yeah," Genny said, eagerly feeding the eager horse. They were certainly two peas in a pod.

"But you don't just eat apples all day every day, right?"

"Ohhhhh…" Genny looked at her, understanding dawning. "Sonny has to eat lots of things, then?"

"Yeah. He needs hay in his diet along with other grains so he gets lots of different nutrients, not just oats all day long."

She thought she'd made Genny understand, but she wasn't appreciating how single-minded she was, until Genny asked, "So, can I feed him hay too? I want to feed him all the food!"

Which made Abby burst out laughing. Genny had been bitten by the horse fever, there was no doubt about it. She was just like Abby had been at her age. She would've slept in her horse's stall each night if her parents would've let her.

"Doc Whitaker has the feeding part under control. He has to make sure that Sonny won't eat too much. Horses will eat and eat and eat until they get sick if you let them." Another trait horses shared with small children.

"Darn," Genny said, her face falling.

Abby helped her pick out a brush and they spent time brushing Sonny's coat to a shine. Thank God Adam had great taste in horses, and Sonny was as gentle and calm as a summer afternoon. He seemed to love Genny's attention almost as much as Genny loved giving it to him.

Yup, Abby was pretty sure she would sleep in Sonny's stall if her parents let her.

After a tearful farewell and more extracted promises about coming back again, Genny left with her harried mother, talking a mile a minute about how you can't just feed horses apples all day long. Which Abby figured was just as good a lesson as any to learn.

She hadn't been able to talk to Wyatt much

that day, which was of course exactly how she wanted it. She wasn't going to spend a lot of time around Wyatt or thinking about Wyatt or talking to Wyatt.

Which meant she should be happy that she hadn't talked to Wyatt much that day. Totally and completely...

Unhappy.

"Hi." His deep voice in her ear surprised her, and she jumped a foot in the air with a startled yelp.

He reached out and put a steadying hand on the small of her back. "Sorry, I didn't mean to surprise you," he said.

Clutching the brush to her chest, she turned towards him with an over-bright smile. "I was just lost in my own little world, I guess. I didn't hear you sneaking up on me."

Sonny had stood placidly in front of them throughout it all, not even shying away when she'd screamed and jumped into the air.

Yeah, Adam had done a real good job picking out horses to work with small children, that was for sure. And jumpy deputies of Long

Valley County. She knew better than to react like that around horses. It could've ended up with a kick to the head around a more skittish horse. But Wyatt…

Did things to her.

Ugh.

She sounded like she was seventeen all over again.

"So how did your day go?" she asked him as they began cleaning up, leading the horses back to their stalls, putting the brushes and feed away.

"Real good. I…" He paused for a moment. "I don't know if I'm about to break a million rules by asking you this, but do you know the story behind Juan? I only know he's in the foster system, but I haven't wanted to ask him why. It just seemed too probing a question to ask a nine-year-old boy."

She nodded slowly as she put the lid back onto the mouse-proof barrels, protecting the oats inside. "I don't know much, other than we arrested both his parents about six months ago. That's a matter of public record – you could find it out if you went and dug up the info in the newspaper. So I'll save you the work and just tell you that his parents were into some bad shit. They were bringing up under-aged girls from Mexico, promising them a new life in the US, and because they were also Mexican, these girls were trusting. And desperate. Then when the girls got here, they were sold. I'm guessing you can imagine what for."

Wyatt's eyes went dark with anger. "Oh Lordy," he whispered.

"Yeah. Even here in Long Valley, we're not exempt from that sort of thing. It's enough to make you sick."

They waved goodbye to Adam who was putting the last of the supplies away for the day, and stepped outside into the weak winter light. The sun was setting; it would be dark soon, and even colder.

"Was Juan a part of any of it, do you know? Did he know what his parents were doing?"

Abby shook her head. "No, not as far as we can tell. They'd drop him off at friends' houses while they did a run. They chose Long Valley because it's so far removed from everywhere; they thought they could fly under the radar. They don't have any family in the US, but thank God they didn't think they ought to bring a small child along for that sort of thing. I don't know if Juan knows even to this day or not."

They slowly walked to Abby's car and she leaned against it, staring out across the frozen fields to the mountains, white with snow and ice, dusky purple around the edges from the setting sun.

"I'm glad Adam is doing this therapy camp," Wyatt said quietly. "Kids like that need someone to give them love and attention and let them know that they matter."

Abby's gaze met his. "There are a lot of kids out there who need that. I know better than most that you're here because you've been court-ordered to do so, but it's still a good cause, nonetheless. I'm glad you picked it."

"Me too," he said simply.

And then they were just staring at each

other and it didn't matter that the cold air was seeping in around the edges of her coat and that her nose was frozen solid and she wasn't sure if she was ever going to be able to feel her toes again. She felt excitement and lust and electricity building up inside of her and her breathing grew shallow and they began leaning, moving, shifting towards each other.

She shouldn't. She really, really, really shouldn't.

And yet, she couldn't stop herself.

Their lips touched, cool and soft and the sparks went shooting through her body and her breath hitched, a shiver running through her. She put her hands up on his broad shoulders, slowly, tentatively. Through her gloves and his winter jacket, she couldn't feel a thing, but still…she was touching him.

His hands settled on her waist and he pulled her forward against him, nestling her between his legs as his hands began stroking up and down her back. Her blood was roaring in her ears and her heart was going a million miles an hour and his tongue, oh his talented tongue was working its way between her lips, exploring, loving…

He pulled back slowly, ever so slowly, and at first she followed him, unwilling to give him up, but finally, she settled back down to the ground and opened up her eyes with a satisfied sigh. He stroked her cheek softly with the pad of his thumb, and she gave him a happy smile.

"I've been wanting to do that for a long time," he said softly.

"I just may have wanted you to do that for a long time," she replied.

He nestled her against him, his arms wrapped around her, holding her tight, as she snuggled her face against his chest. It was cold and she should want to get into her car and turn on the heater, but she wanted to be snuggled against Wyatt more. Ignore the world for just a few moments.

"Sierra would've loved this camp," Wyatt said, out of the blue. "She got horse fever so young; I'm not kidding you – it was her second word. Right after 'nana' which meant 'banana.' She didn't learn Mom or Dad for quite a while, which just shows you where her priorities were."

Abby felt the happiness inside of her slowly leak away, like a balloon with a pin-sized hole in it.

Sierra.

Wyatt's baby girl who died when she was only five. The daughter he misses so much, he wants more children more than anything else in the world.

She felt the panic begin to grow in the pit of her stomach and spread up and out. She had to go. She had to go right then. She had to leave.

"Igottagohome," she said in a burst, whirled out of his arms, and slipped into her car, starting it and throwing it into gear before taking off down the long, rutted dirt road back to the county road into town.

She was an idiot. A first-class dumbass.

But even now, she couldn't quite make herself regret that kiss.

CHAPTER 27

WYATT

THE NEXT MORNING found Wyatt in the shop, working on random shit. He was mostly cleaning up. Months of neglect meant a whole lot of spider webs, and he didn't really have the concentration to do anything too strenuous, anyway.

The only thing his brain wanted to focus on was that kiss.

Well, and her reaction afterward. Why did she take off like that? Was he scaring her by wanting too much too quickly?

He mindlessly shoved wrenches and screwdrivers into the drawers of his toolbox as he replayed the conversation in his head. He had no idea what caused her to bolt like that. She knew he had a daughter. She knew Sierra had died in that car wreck at the hands of that bastard who couldn't figure out when enough was enough.

So why that reaction?

He broke from his memories long enough to notice that he'd cleared the entire workbench. It looked…nice. It wouldn't stay looking like this come spring, but for the moment, he took pride in how uncluttered it was.

Huh. Uncluttered, but damn dusty. He looked around for the broom and finally spotted it in the corner.

"Some cleaning tool you are," he said out loud to himself as he crossed the shop. "You have more dust on you than the damn floor." Oh well. It wasn't like he was going to be able to make his shop spic-and-span. Less dirt on the floor overall was a win.

He'd just made the first couple of pushes of the broom when he heard the crunching of tires on the snow-covered gravel drive outside.

His head spun and his heart jumped a little. He had very few visitors out to his place, and even less after he'd been locked up for so long, which meant that the chances were real high that it was Abby out there. His heart went into double-time.

He had to play it cool. Damn, was he sixteen again?

The gravel gave a tortured crunch as the vehicle came to a stop by the house. He debated going out and flagging her down.

No, no. He kept sweeping the floor. A guy didn't want to seem *too* eager.

He pushed the broom a couple more times mindlessly and then began to wonder if she'd think to come over to the shop to look for him. Maybe he should go out and flag her down after all.

He leaned the broom back in the corner where he'd found it and was just about to head outside when he heard the vehicle restart and crunch its way over to the shop.

The car door opened and closed, and then the shop door swung open. He opened his mouth to say hi when he heard, "What're you doing hiding in here?"

The person was framed by the light coming in from outside, and it didn't look a damn thing like Abby's curves. And then there was also the fact that he'd recognize Stetson's voice anywhere.

Dammit.

"I hadn't had a chance to clean since I got out, so I thought I'd give it a little attention." There was an edge to Wyatt's tone that he really didn't like, but couldn't seem to stop from appearing. Even when he was trying to be nice to Stetson, his body just seemed to be allergic to the idea.

"Not much going on around the farm?" Stetson asked.

"Not during the winter," he got out. Yup, that was definitely snappier than he'd meant for it to be. But truly, Stetson should know that not much farming was done during the winter. It was kind of a dumbass comment to make.

Tension filled the shop as they just stared at

each other. Finally, Stetson lifted his hat and ran his fingers through his hair in frustration.

"So I don't know if you can or if you want to, but Jennifer and I are hosting a gender announcement party for the baby in a couple of weeks. Jennifer wanted me to ask you to come. If you can."

The last line came out harder than Wyatt thought it needed to, but he took a deep breath. *I guess I deserve a* little *backlash. Even if I don't like it.*

"That'd be nice. My probation allows me to leave the farm, so I can't imagine why I couldn't make it over," he said slowly. "How's Jennifer doing?"

"She's doing pretty good," Stetson said, a smile starting to form. Finally, a topic he was happy to discuss. "She knows what we're having and has been a pest with all of her teasing."

"You didn't ask her what it was?" Wyatt was confused.

"Nope. I wanted to be surprised along with everyone else." Stetson grinned, the first genuine smile he'd sent Wyatt's way in…well, way too long.

"That's good to hear," Wyatt said. And it was. He wasn't sure what else to say, though. Conversations had never flowed easily between them. Punches? Yes. Honest-to-God conversations? Not so much. "Uhhh…thanks for the invitation."

"Sure," Stetson said as he turned back toward the door.

Wyatt watched his retreating back for a few steps.

"Hey," he called out, stopping Stetson in his tracks. "Declan said you helped keep things going around here during harvest time. I'm sure that wasn't easy, especially while getting married, too, and dealing with your own harvest."

Stetson turned and stared at him. The muscle in his jaw jumped as he prepared himself for whatever he expected Wyatt to say or do next.

"I just wanted to say thank you," Wyatt finished.

Stetson's eyebrows practically hit his hairline and he continued to stare at Wyatt, as if waiting for the other shoe to drop. When Wyatt didn't say anything else, he finally just nodded, mumbled something about it being no problem, and headed out the door.

Wyatt heaved a sigh when the door closed behind his youngest brother. Every conversation with him was a field of landmines. He never knew if he was going to step in it and blow things to kingdom come again or not.

On the other hand, they'd just managed to have a whole conversation without any punching or yelling, and that had to be some sort of record. Oh, and a genuine smile from Stetson. That *was* a record.

Wyatt's happiness was short-lived, though, as he began to ruminate over the choices Stetson had made in his life.

As usual, when Stetson had screwed up, he'd been saved by someone else – this time, the saving came in the form of a gorgeous banker. Only Stetson would be lucky enough to be sent a beautiful, young, single banker who was smart enough to push him to sell off his wheat and save his farm. The Miller Family Farm that had been in the Miller family for five generations.

It only took Stetson one damn year to put it at risk of ending up on the auction block.

Wyatt began coughing up a storm and realized that he'd begun swinging the broom recklessly, throwing more dirt into the air than into the dirt pile.

Being upset about everything that Stetson gets handed to him doesn't help you or hurt him. He doesn't know you feel that way, so it really doesn't matter to him. All it does is hurt you and keep you from focusing on what you can change.

The discussion he and Rhonda had had at his last appointment rang in his ears. He hated to admit that she was right, because it all just sounded so mumbo-jumbo to him — forgive Stetson and move on. Shouldn't Stetson have to pay for being a little shithead his entire life?

But as he coughed and sneezed, leaning on the broom handle to keep himself upright, he knew the counselor was right. Stetson didn't know and probably didn't care that Wyatt was angry that he got everything in life that he wanted, including a little baby to call his own. He didn't have everything taken away from him in an instant like Wyatt had.

And sure, maybe it'd be better for all involved if Wyatt just let it go. But as he began sweeping, a little less emphatically this time, he couldn't help thinking that that was easier said than done.

CHAPTER 28

ABBY

ABBY PULLED UP in front of Wyatt's home. Her family's home, before the bank took it all away.

It was still weird to see it a sage green, so different from the white her mom had liked. She knew that time went on, and Shelly, Wyatt's wife, had had every right to paint her house whatever color she wanted.

It still seemed a little sacrilegious to Abby, but then again, her and Dad had basically turned everything her mom ever touched into a shrine. And maybe that wasn't healthy either.

She looked over at the tire swing hanging

from the oak tree's branches, swaying slightly in the cold winter winds. Abby had spent so many summer days on that tire swing, stretching her legs up to the sky, just sure that if she pumped her legs hard enough, she'd be able to flip all the way over the top of the branch and down the other side.

Okay. Enough stalling.

It was time to get out and talk to Wyatt. With a deep breath, she got out into the cold air, bracing herself against the wind, and hurried up to the front porch. She knocked lightly and then huddled against the door, her eyes automatically picking out the changes to her childhood home. They'd replaced the street numbers with fancier, more expensive metal numbers and the mailbox was—

The door opened. "Oh, hey," Wyatt said, the surprise evident on his face. "Come in."

He mumbled something about two visitors in one day, but when she said, "What?" he waved the question away.

"What's going on? Is everything okay?" he asked, a panicked note in his voice.

It took her a moment but she finally put the pieces together of why he sounded panicked. Of course. The last time a county police officer showed up at his door, his wife and child were dead on the side of the road. Even though she was off-duty, he had no way of knowing that. She was still in her deputy uniform.

"No, everything is fine," she said. "I came over straight from work – I'm not even on the clock right now."

"Oh. Good." His face relaxed into a full smile. "You want something to drink? I have water, lemonade, coffee, probably a soda or two…"

"No, no. Listen, I need to tell you something." She drew in a breath, one that she could feel all the way to her toes. "I need to tell you…I can't have kids." The words were the barest of a whisper, barely audible above the sound of the central heating system pumping out warm air, but they might as well have been shouted in the middle of town square. They landed like a bomb between them, separating them forever. A chasm that could never be crossed.

"What?" he breathed, staring at her.

"When I was a kid…I fell off the merry-go-round, right onto someone's bike. The pedals…" She made a gesture towards her stomach. "They had to do emergency surgery on me to patch everything back up, but the doctors said that the damage to my uterus was too great. I would never be able to have kids. I went to an OB-GYN about a year ago just to make sure, and they ran all sorts of tests on me. There's just not enough room for a baby, after they took out the damaged tissue."

She held her breath and just stared at him. It was damn awkward, bringing this up with him. It wasn't like they were really even dating, right? They'd just kissed that one time.

But if what he was feeling on his end was anywhere close to what she was feeling on her end…she had to tell him. He had to know before this went any further. Because if her gut was right, he wouldn't want it to go any further.

Yup, he'd shut down. His face, open and

happy and welcoming, had become a brick wall of…nothingness. He shoved his hands out towards her, fists facing her. "See any blood on my knuckles?" he rasped.

Startled, she look down and stared at his knuckles. "Nooo…"

"Then you can report back to your father that I haven't been beating anyone up lately. Now get the hell out of my house."

She jerked her head back, her eyes spiking with hot, painful tears. She didn't say anything. Couldn't say anything. She spun around and felt blindly for the doorknob, yanking the door open and stumbling out into the cold winter air, burning in her lungs and she was running, stumbling, towards her cruiser, crawling inside, shoving the key into the ignition and pulling away, the tears running unchecked down her cheeks.

CHAPTER 29

WYATT

HE WAS A CLASS-A ASSHOLE.

He knew it, Stetson knew it, hell, Declan probably knew it and was just too nice to say so.

And now Abby knew it.

Oh, she probably had her inklings, considering the fact that he'd once punched her father and laid him out flat on the ground, and because he'd spent seven weeks in her close company because of charges of assault and battery.

But somehow, she'd overlooked all of that.

Somehow, she hadn't seemed to notice, or at least hold it against him.

But not now. There was no way that she missed this fact now.

It'd been three days since her announcement. Three days of hell. Only one day of working with the kids out at Adam's place, and all anyone seemed to want to know was where was Abby? The little brown-haired girl who always clung to Abby like her shadow had been especially insistent.

"She promised she was going to come again!" she'd said, her mouth full of metal making it hard for her to speak clearly. But what she wanted to say wasn't lost on Wyatt. She was a force of nature, and her wishes were crystal clear.

"I'm not sure where she's at," Wyatt had said lamely. Abby'd actually never planned on coming that day; it interfered with her work schedule. But he couldn't tell the little girl that and lead her on, making her believe that Abby would for sure be there the next time. He rather doubted it, actually…

"Did you make her sad?" the little girl had demanded, crossing her arms and glaring at Wyatt.

Dammit. Even small children seemed to know that he'd screwed this up.

But on the other hand, he'd told Abby how much he wanted kids, way back during Christmas. She'd known all this time what children meant to him. She'd had a whole month to tell him, and hadn't. The people around him were always betraying him; he couldn't rely on anyone to tell him the truth when it didn't suit their needs.

Shit. That wasn't true, and he knew it. At least not when it came to Abby.

His head thunked forward against the tractor seat. He was out in the shop, ostensibly doing a tuneup on this old workhorse, but he'd spent the last…he didn't know how long, actually, just staring off into space.

With a grunt, he left the shop and headed over to the barn. He was going to spend time with Elvis. At least *he* still liked Wyatt. Maggie

Mae pushed herself up onto her feet and trotted alongside him as he went.

"*When* was she supposed to tell me?" he asked Maggie, who gave him a mournful yip in return.

That's what was getting stuck in his craw. He wanted to just hate her because she hadn't told him the truth from the beginning, but what beginning, exactly, was that? When he was first thrown in jail? Was she just supposed to tell every inmate who came through, on the off-chance that they fell in love during their stay?

He entered the warmish barn, the heater on low to keep the cold at bay. Flakes were swirling again; another winter storm was going to hit. Even for Long Valley, this had been a hell of a winter.

Elvis nickered when he saw Wyatt, his ears pricking up. Maggie Mae headed straight to her blanket in the corner so she could get back to her interrupted nap. She flopped down with a disgruntled sigh.

Wyatt ignored the pain Maggie obviously felt she'd just been put through, and instead grabbed a metal scoop and opened up the mice-proof bin of oats to dish some out. He dumped it into the feeding bucket and carried it over to Elvis, who began hoovering it down like he hadn't seen food in the last ten years. Which was *always* how he ate oats; that and carrots. Wyatt long ago stopped worrying that he was mistakenly starving his horse. The big glutton just loved to eat.

"I treated her like shit," he said, stroking his hand down Elvis' neck as he continued to lip around the bottom of the bucket, attempting to suck up the last bits of grain. "I couldn't figure out why she'd run away that day when we'd kissed, and now I know.

"You could say that she should've told me then, but…" He paused, staring at the far wall of the barn, seeing nothing. "That's the kind of private information that you just don't go around telling every soul in sight, and it probably took her time to build up her courage to talk to me."

Just like it'd taken him time – three days, to be exact – to be able to see the situation clearly.

She'd gathered up her courage, told him the truth, and he'd promptly acted like the bastard he was. He was never going to win a personality contest, but even for him, his behavior that day had been inexcusable.

Elvis, the oats officially gone, began nibbling on Wyatt's jacket instead. Wyatt pushed him away with a small laugh. "I better go ride you before you start eating your stall door." Elvis just nickered again, obviously trying to prove his innocence of such charges.

Wyatt didn't believe him, not one bit.

He saddled him up and they headed outside into the cold, blowing snow, Maggie Mae fast on their heels. This would be good for all of them; Maggie needed to get outside and stretch her legs too. He looked down and saw her loping alongside him, tongue lolling out, happy as a clam.

He steered Elvis towards the trees that ran along his fence line that separated him from Mr. Krein, his nearest neighbor. He'd follow the frozen creek along. It was beautiful, winter or summer, and the view always soothed him.

As they trotted along, Wyatt turned the thought over and over in his mind. It was pretty clear to all involved, even him, that he needed to beg Abby's forgiveness for his behavior the other day. She'd never been anything but thoughtful and sweet to him, and didn't deserve what he said, not one bit.

But that didn't solve the other, looming question: Could he fall in love with someone who couldn't give him what he wanted most in the world? He wanted kids. He wanted someone to have his smile and his wife's temperament (because God only knows, this world couldn't handle two Wyatts in it). He wanted someone to teach how to catch a baseball, and dance with on her wedding day, and show just how to make the perfect weld, and how to curry a horse just right.

He wanted to make a difference in a kid's life, girl or boy, he didn't care. He wanted someone to call him Dad.

His throat felt tight with unshed tears. He hadn't cried since the night Shelly and Sierra died. Not at the funeral, not a day since.

But the idea of losing the ability to have kids…that was a hell of a price to pay to love someone. Could he love Abby enough to forgive her? Not her, but the situation? It wasn't fair to her to be in love with someone who would always resent her for keeping the one thing he wanted away from him.

Love…

Had he meant to use that word? He thought back to the last couple of months. Even in the depths of inmate hell, the one shining moment had been Abby. When she'd walk by and they'd trade joking insults or just brief comments. It was what had kept him sane while being locked in a 6x9 jail cell. Unlike so many others in the community, she hadn't judged him and found him wanting.

And then, they'd kissed. And his whole world shifted on its axis and he wasn't sure what he wanted or who he was anymore.

His eyes stung from the cold winter air; nothing more than that. He dashed at them with the back of his hand.

He had a choice to make, and in deference

to Abby and her feelings, he needed to make it soon. Before he'd screwed everything up, they'd made plans for him to pick her up tomorrow and take her out to Adam's. He had no idea if she still wanted him to, or if he wanted to.

He better start making decisions.

He wiped at his eyes again.

Damn winter air.

CHAPTER 30

ABBY

ABBY STARED AT HER BOWL of breakfast cereal in front of her, pushing the soggy Corn Flakes around the bowl mindlessly. She was supposed to go out to Adam's place today. She was supposed to hang out with Genny and the horses and of course, see Wyatt.

Wyatt, who hated her guts, all because of something she had no control over. Did he think she *enjoyed* falling onto the bike and wrecking her stomach, and any chance of a normal adulthood? She'd known since elementary school that she didn't get to fall in love. She didn't get to get married. No one would love someone like her, who couldn't have children.

She kinda wondered if that wasn't why she became a police officer. Sure, her dad needed the help at the county; when he was elected, it was a contentious election and the county police officers at the time had all backed the incumbent. The day her father had been sworn into office, 90% of the police force quit en masse in protest. She'd basically been pressed into service, went through the Idaho Police Academy training as quickly as possible, and had been at the Long Valley County Jail ever since.

Things had settled down, and her dad probably could've stood for her to quit and move onto something else. It'd been years since that first election, and the county had finally coalesced around him. So why hadn't she quit?

Because a police officer was scary. No one expected a police officer — a *female* one, no less — to find love and get married. It was okay if she was single; no one expected otherwise.

When it came to dating, it was bad enough

that her father was the sheriff; that probably would've scared off most of the men all by it-self. But a female police officer just didn't get many offers for dates, unless she started counting drunken propositions, which she most certainly was not.

So yeah, she'd been using the police badge as a shield for her heart all this time. Better to keep men at bay than to allow them in, and risk getting hurt because of her…inadequacies.

She closed her eyes with a groan. Maybe what she was thinking was true, but that didn't make it any more wonderful. It was a fine thing to figure out something like this about herself after all this time. She wasn't sure what to do with the knowledge; truth was, even if being a police officer had been a subconscious shield against the world, it had obviously failed with a certain Wyatt Miller. When she hadn't been looking, he'd snuck in and stole her heart.

She heard lapping noises and opened up her eyes to see Jasmine drinking the milk in her cereal bowl.

"You little beggar," she said, laughing. Jasmine flicked her tail but kept drinking it up. Nothing short of taking the bowl away from her would scare Jasmine into leaving a prize as fine as this. Not when there was milk on the line.

Ten minutes. Wyatt was supposed to be at her house in ten minutes, but there was no chance he was actually going to show up, right? She was probably going to see him at the courthouse when he turned in his paperwork, and occasionally around town after that, but he wasn't coming to her house today to pick her up. He hated her, for something she didn't control, want, or desire.

Which brought her right back to where she'd started.

Finally satiated, Jasmine sat back on her haunches and began cleaning her face, giving herself a studious bath. Right on the dining room table.

"You are so spoiled," Abby said, picking Jasmine up and carrying her to the couch. "Please stay off the dining room table. I need to have *some* standards, you know." Jasmine gave her a haughty look, dissatisfied at being moved, and then stalked to the end of the couch where she settled down and began giving herself a proper bath.

Rolling her eyes at her spoiled rotten cat – because of course it was someone else's fault for spoiling her, not Abby's – she began cleaning off the dining room table. She'd need to scrub it down after Jasmine sat her ass on—

Ding-dong.

Abby straightened up and looked at the door.

Surely not. Wyatt wouldn't come, right? He pretty much hated her guts. He wasn't going to come pick her up so she could go spend time *not* talking to him. Because there was no way he wanted to talk to her. Not after…

Ding-dong.

She hurried to the front door, shoving her hair out of her face as she went. She was in an old faded flannel shirt and oversized sweat pants. She hadn't exactly wanted Wyatt to see her like this.

Why does it matter? He doesn't like you anyway.

Still wasn't useful for her self-esteem.

With a sigh, she opened the door to find a nervous-as-hell-looking Wyatt standing there.

"Hey," she said softly.

"Hey." He swallowed hard. "Can I come in for a minute?"

"Sure." She swung the door open wide so he could come walking in. She wanted to say something sarcastic, like, "But only if you promise not to be an asshole," but decided against it.

"I wanted to apologize," Wyatt said, turning around to look at her. Jasmine came walking over and began nudging his leg, looking for affection.

"Then apologize," Abby snapped.

Maybe her temper wasn't quite under control as much as she thought it was.

He stared at her. "What?"

"You said you wanted to apologize, not that you *were* apologizing. If you want to, I suggest you do."

She crossed her arms over her chest and glared at him. Jasmine had looked adorable enough to convince Wyatt to pick her up, and she was busy purring in his arms with happiness at the attention she was getting.

Cheater.

Her cat should only be loyal to Abby, but alas, she was loyal to anyone who petted her.

Wyatt cleared his throat and started again. "Abby, I am apologizing." He looked her straight in the eye and continued, "I apologize for being a jackass to you the other day. You came over to tell me the truth, and I acted totally inappropriately. It's not your fault that you can't have children, and instead of showing you understanding, I ripped into you. I never should have, and I have no excuse for it. Please know that I am sorry."

He was staring at her, his dark blue eyes haunted and worried. She knew Wyatt. She knew that he'd apologized – and meant it – maybe once or twice in his whole life.

He meant it now.

And that meant a lot to her.

"Thank you," she said, her voice coming out tight and high. A part of her wanted to cry, but she'd been around men her whole life. The fastest way to completely freak a guy out was to turn on the water works. She swallowed the lump in her throat down instead.

"So where does that leave us?" she asked. The question hung over them like a mist over a gloomy forest. They couldn't go anywhere; they couldn't move on, until they figured that question out.

He shrugged. "I don't know if I'm ready to answer that question yet. I understand if that means that you don't want to be around me. I'm asking you to take a chance on me when I don't know what I want yet. These past four days have been hell on earth. I've been damn miserable since I threw you out of my house."

"Good," she said, and stuck her tongue out at him.

He let out a startled laugh and said, "I guess I deserve that." Jasmine, Traitor of the First Order, had completely melted into Wyatt, stretched out so far in his arms, Abby was a little afraid she'd just plop right out and fall on the floor. Wyatt was stroking her from head to ass, and Jasmine was purring up a storm.

"I've known you my whole life, Abby. But until that night at the convenience store, I didn't actually *know* you. You were just someone closer to Declan's age than mine, and I always had my own thing going. I can't pretend that not having kids is a small thing to me. It's a huge deal. But these past four days have shown me that you are a huge deal to me, too. Will you give me the time to figure this out?"

"I can't have you resenting me for the rest of my life, Wyatt Miller. That isn't fair to me. If you choose me, you choose me knowing what you've chosen. I can't have it any other way. I can't have someone in my life who resents me for circumstances beyond my control."

"I know." He gently put Jasmine down on the couch and with a disgruntled sniff, she began giving herself a bath. Wyatt moved to stand directly in front of Abby, picking up her hands in his and staring at her intently. "I need time. I'm not ready for that discussion. Not yet. Give me time to sort myself out. Don't give up on me yet. I also can't decide that being with you is worth giving up the dream of having kids, if I don't really know you. Not like I should. I know that you have a terrific laugh and a forgiving heart and you're a hell of a kisser. And that your cat is just about the most adorable thing I've ever laid eyes on. But I don't know *you*, not yet, and I need to. Before I take that next step."

She stared at him solemnly for a long moment. "Fair enough," she said. "I appreciate you being honest with me and telling me how things stand. Just know that I won't always be okay with how things are right now. Eventually, you'll have to shit or get off the pot."

Wyatt threw his head back and laughed. "Fair enough," he said, echoing her words. "Now, are you gonna come with me to Adam's place? That little girl with the braids − I think she thinks I drove you off. Last time, she did nothing but interrogate me about where you were at."

"Did you tell her that you drove me off?"

Abby said tartly, turning to her bedroom to get dressed.

"Oh hell no. I wasn't sure I'd live through that revelation."

"You always scared of nine-year-old girls with pigtails?" she asked saucily, standing in the doorway of her bedroom.

"Just on days that end with Y," he volleyed back.

She shot him a grin, her first true smile since he showed up. "Let me get dressed and then we can head out. We shouldn't be late for your community service hours; I hear your probation officer is a real hard ass."

"The worst!" he shouted at her through the closed bedroom door. She grinned to herself. They were back to normal-ish again. And right then, she was willing to grab onto that with both hands.

CHAPTER 31

WYATT

*L*IFE AROUND ABBY was maddeningly wonderful. Horribly amazing. Stupendously awful.

All of that and more.

They'd settled into a routine; when she wasn't working at the courthouse or out on patrol, he'd come pick her up and drive her out to Adam's place. They'd laugh and chat the whole way out there, and then go their separate ways once they arrived. Abby had a group of kids who loved her and anytime she wasn't able to make it out there, they spent the whole time whining to anyone who would listen about it.

Not that he could blame them. Without Abby there, there was no sunshine. There was no happiness. Which seemed utterly dramatic and over the top to him, but also damn true.

Rhonda told him the other day that he was happier than she'd seen him since she'd started working with him. Which was also true. He *wanted* to smile now, which wasn't something he could've necessarily said before. It was, to be quite honest, a totally new experience.

He and Jorge spent some time pouring over seed catalogs and discussing the newest weed killers on the market. Sometimes, they had to get one of his grandkids in to help with the finer points of their discussion, but they got things figured out. He was as set as he was ever going to be for the new season. He even went down to the credit union and signed the paperwork to borrow the money for that season's operating expenses, to get that step out of the way.

He'd done all he could do, and now it was just time to wait for spring to arrive.

And wait for Stetson's party to arrive.

He was kinda surprised by how much he was looking forward to it. If his parents had still been around, they would've been hitting the roof, thrilled to pieces at the idea of a new grandchild to welcome into the family. They'd done that once before…

He swallowed the pain down. Now wasn't the time to get wrapped up in memories. He had Juan here, wanting to know how to get a bridle over a horse's head without them trying to shimmy back out of it, and he had Abby over by Sonny, sending him lascivious glances through her eyelashes and…

He had a life to live. Not one to pine over in the rearview mirror, but to live *today*.

He couldn't remember the last time he felt that way.

And it was a damn good feeling.

"Hold on, Juan, you've got to hold the bit in this hand, see?" he said, rescuing the bridle from his young charge's hands and rearranging it. He helped Juan get up onto the step stool.

"All right, now start by sliding this into his mouth…"

Yeah, he had a lot to live for right now.

CHAPTER 32

ABBY

*I*T'D BEEN A LONG DAY. A long-ass day, to be specific. Mr. Krein down at the library had gotten riled up over his overdue fines – again – and the head librarian had called for help – again – and after she'd gotten Mr. Krein settled down and willing to pay his fines, which was quite the feat if she did say so herself, all she wanted to do was go home and settle into a hot tub of bubbles and read. She ought to read a thriller set in the Middle East, since she just negotiated a peace as tricky as finding one in the Middle East would be, but before she could decide which author to pick up that evening, she heard her father hollering her name.

Dammit.

She walked from the front office area back to the sheriff's office. She'd take offense and tell him to stop hollering at her like she was a little child, but he did it with all of the officers, not just her. This wasn't a case of him not seeing her as an adult, but rather just a case of him being…him.

"Yes?" she asked, in an overly sweet tone of voice in the doorway of his office. He glared at her, catching the sarcasm dripping off her voice and not liking it one bit.

"Close the door behind you!" he barked.

A tiny part of her wished she had enough guts to walk out into the hallway and then pull the door closed behind her, but she was pretty sure she wouldn't live through such shenanigans, so with a sigh, she stepped fully into his office and shut the door behind her.

"Yes?" she repeated again, just as sweetly.

He glared at her just as hard, but she simply looked back him, waiting for him to speak. Finally, he barked, "The rumor all over town is that *my daughter* is spending hours on end with a guy on parole here in this county. I—"

"Are you talking as my dad right now or my boss?" she interrupted. He stopped, his mouth gaping open.

"Your boss," he finally ground out.

"Then I suggest you refer to me as your deputy, not as your daughter," she said. She wasn't yelling; she wasn't snarky. She was simply pointing out information.

"My deputy," he snarled, "is spending copious amounts of time with the town ruffian, who gets in more fights than Muhammad Ali. Is *that* better?"

"*Your deputy* is spending time with small children with learning disabilities, or children in the foster care system, teaching them responsibility and how to work with animals. A man on parole happens to be picking me up and dropping me off, but there is nothing more to it than that." The one kiss they'd shared flashed through her mind, but she pushed it away.

Nothing had happened since then, and for all she knew, nothing ever would. They hadn't mentioned children or their future again after he'd come to her house that one day, and she had to face the fact that they may be "just friends" for the rest of her life. "What I do in my free time, especially if I choose to spend it doing community service, is none of my *employer's* business."

"Wyatt Miller is nothing but trouble," her dad exploded, "and you know it! First, you pushed the line by volunteering to be his parole officer, but to actually go work with him while he's serving his community service hours…it's beyond the pale, Abby, and you know it."

"You're so damned sure he's nothing but a screw-up," Abby hissed, leaning forward on her father's desk, planting her fists as she stared up at him, "that you've never bothered to get to know him. Maybe if you had, you'd have a different take on the situation."

"He punched me!" Her father slammed his fist into the palm of his hand to emphasize the words. "There's no denying th—"

"His wife and daughter were lying on the side of the road, Dad. What did you expect him to do – stop and ask politely if he could come through?"

"He was getting in the way of the EMTs. If he really cared that much about saving their lives, he would've let them work without interference."

"Lordy, Dad, are you *really* that cold-hearted?" She stared at him in disbelief. "You *really* think that Wyatt, in the most awful moment of his life, was supposed to rationally assess the situation and decide what the best course of action was?"

"I would!" her father volleyed back. "I know better than to get in the way of the people trying to save those I love!"

"And you're a trained officer, for hell's sakes, Dad. Wyatt is not. He's just a sugar beet farmer. He doesn't know how to react in situations where his family is dying in front of his eyes. It's time to cut him some slack. Let's talk about what's really bothering you – that comment he made in the bar, about running the farm better than you." Her dad flinched, and she knew she was right; his bluster about what Wyatt did and did not do on the side of the road was a cover for what was really bothering him: Wyatt hurting his pride in front of the entire community. "Did you ever happen to *talk* to him about what happened that night?"

"Why the hell would I go and do a thing like that? I'm not about to give him another chance to tell me what a screw-up he thinks I am, and—"

"Or you could have a completely different interaction with him than that, Dad." She glared at him, all of her frustration on behalf of Wyatt showing through. She wasn't holding back – she was fighting for the one person in town who had no one to fight for him. The one person everyone thought didn't need a champion.

But everyone needed a champion. Even prickly farmers named Wyatt Miller.

"If you are sleeping with the guy," her dad said, voice low as he too leaned forward, staring her down, "then just tell me. No need to try to make him sound better than he really is or make excuses for him. It's time to own up to the choices you're making, Abigail."

Her head snapped back at that. Her father rarely called her Abigail, and when he did… well, it was safe to say that it wasn't a good sign.

Abby suddenly felt deep empathy for Wyatt. To fight against this kind of deep-seated antipathy over and over again, for years on end… no wonder he'd withdrawn into himself. Sure, he didn't make it easy to love him at times, and he'd made more than his fair share of mistakes. But this refusal to see him as anything but a monster…it had to be exhausting.

Something inside of her snapped. Snapped into pieces and she began grinning. Her father stared at her, slowly pulling back as her grin grew wider. "Wha…?"

"I just realized how freeing it is to not give a damn. No wonder Wyatt never does. Sheriff Connelly, the truth is, my shift ended ten minutes ago and I want to go home. Unless you actually have something to hold over my head, which I am quite sure you don't or you would've told me already, you cannot stop me from hanging out with Wyatt Miller seven days a week. Hell, you can't stop me from sleeping with the man. Damn, if I'm going to be accused of it, I might as well, right? Goodnight, sir." And on that note, she spun on her heel and stalked out of the office, down the hallway, out the doors, into the weak winter sunlight, over to her cruiser, and hopped inside.

It felt good, damn good, to stand up to her dad. She pulled out of the parking lot, her tires squealing, her grin stretching from ear to ear. Her whole life, she'd always tried to please others. She'd done everything she could to keep the peace. She'd listened to her father, even when he was wrong. She'd done her best to make everyone happy.

Now, it was time to make her happy.

CHAPTER 33

WYATT

*H*E HEARD A VEHICLE crunching on the gravel outside and cocked his head to the side wonderingly. Who was here? Was Stetson here to argue with him again? Was Declan here to try to convince him that Stetson really was a sweetie after all? Declan always was one for impossible goals.

A car door slammed, boots on the front porch, and Wyatt reached over to click off the TV and pushed himself out of his recliner. Whoever it was, was in a hur—

His front door swung open.

"What the hell?" he said, and then he realized it was Abby. She was walking straight over to him and he just stared at her in shock. She was in her uniform and she had a real weird look on her face. Maybe this time, it really was something that had gone wrong – maybe Declan was hurt in an accident or—

She wrapped her hands around his head and pulled him to her, shoving her tongue into his mouth. Forceful, demanding, she pulled back and said, "If I'm gonna be accused of sleeping with you, I might as well be doing it." She grabbed his hand and began dragging him towards the staircase, up to the second story.

A tiny part of his brain wondered for a moment how she knew where his bedroom was, but then remembered all over again – duh. She used to live here. Of course she'd know where the master bedroom was.

"Is there something going on that I ought to know about?" he asked, his mind whirling as they took the stairs two at a time. Not that he was going to complain about finally having a break in his dry spell, but it seemed like a good idea to figure out what was going on in that head of hers.

"Yeah, I live in a tiny town that thinks every little thing that happens is their business. If they're going to get up in my business, then I should at least give them something to get up into, dontcha think?"

And with that, she shoved Wyatt backward onto his bed.

CHAPTER 34

ABBY

*A*BBY ADVANCED ON HIM, noting the shocked expression on his face with pride. The look, the twinkle in his eyes and the small upward turn of the corner of his lips told her that the shock in his eyes was the product of being taken off guard, not of fear or anger.

Good.

Abby didn't bother with any of her clothes. The moment was too raw. This was about her getting what she wanted.

Something in the back of her mind tingled, reminding her that this wasn't completely fair to Wyatt, because what she wanted in that moment was to tell everyone to go to hell. She knew she should feel guilty for using him this way, but no matter how hard she tried, she just couldn't make herself care.

Her hands were on board with her hastily created plan and were fumbling with Wyatt's belt buckle, and then the button of his jeans and zipper.

With a hearty tug, she pulled the waistband of his pants and his underwear down far enough that she could reach under the fabric and free him. Her fingers wrapped around his shaft and she realized that it was perfect. *He* was perfect. Okay, a little on the large side, but then again, so was she. She was *pretty* sure he'd fit inside of her. She decided to start with her mouth and see how it fit, and then go from there.

She positioned herself between his knees, Wyatt spreading open wide to accommodate her service belt and other police paraphernalia. A part of her knew that she should at least take the time to get her service belt off, but it was a very small part of her and she ignored it with impunity, instead dropping her head forward and opening her mouth. Her lips slid around the head of Wyatt's dick. He let out a moaning sigh of relief – the obvious celebration of the end of a very long self-imposed dry spell.

She grinned to herself, officially dismissing any guilt that she might be using him. Maybe she was, but he was happy to be used, so that was good enough for her.

Abby slid her lips down the shaft until the tip of his cock touched the back of her throat. She pulled back, dragging her lips along his skin, enjoying the heat emanating from him. She pushed her head downward again, re-tracing the path she'd just taken. She drew in a deep breath through her nose, the musky scent speaking to her mind of shared desire.

The hasty nature of what was happening along with her uncharacteristically dominant attitude made sucking Wyatt's cock feel deli-ciously…naughty.

She wasn't as innocent as the freshly driven snow. She'd been with other men before; not one given to impulsive sexual desires or one-night stands, every man before Wyatt had been somebody she was dating. Each time she'd been with a man, it'd been because she'd had feelings for that person. She'd done this before, as an expression of attraction and what she'd thought of at the time as love.

This time was different. This time, it wasn't a planned event with a long-term boyfriend; it was spontaneous and hot and rough and…just what she needed.

She pulled her head back, letting him escape her mouth, her lips making a popping sound as it did so. She didn't realize that she'd been so forceful in her suction. Wyatt gasped at the sudden change.

Abby sprung to her feet and began tearing at the buckle of her gun-belt, letting it drop the moment that the buckle freed itself. The heavy leather combined with the weight of all of her equipment caused a loud thud to echo through the room as it hit the floor.

"You'd better get those clothes off quickly," she ordered Wyatt, her voice heavy and breathy. Wyatt didn't say anything but instead began quickly unbuttoning his shirt. Abby continued her frantic undressing. She hastily pulled at the shoelaces of her heavy boots. She momentarily cursed the heavy utilitarian footwear for being both completely unsexy and difficult to remove in a hurry.

Finally having negotiated the knots of her shoelaces, she stood back up and simultaneously kicked at the heels of the boots and fumbled with the enclosure of her uniform pants. She did this all by feel while her eyes focused on Wyatt's bare chest.

Sculpted angular lines of his work-hardened muscles, covered by a scattering of hair, caught the light streaming through the window. His body seemed to glint and glow as his chest rose and fell.

She'd never seen a more gorgeous sight in her life.

Somehow, she managed to free her feet from the boots and her legs from the pants just as Wyatt flung his shirt across the room. Her fingers immediately began working on the buttons of her own shirt while Wyatt shoved his pants and underwear down his legs. As his hands pushed the fabric lower, Abby watched the tightly toned muscles of his thighs ripple as he held himself off the mattress.

She wanted him. All of him.

Abby flung her shirt off and immediately began pulling at the Velcro straps holding her vest in place. *This crap takes forever to get off.* Wyatt was completely naked and she hadn't even gotten to her underwear yet.

Really not fair.

She picked up the pace, dropping the heavy bulletproof vest to the ground before yanking her black could-not-be-less-sexy sports bra over her head.

Wyatt had propped himself up on his elbows to watch her stripping.

Despite the pervasiveness of Halloween costumes that might fool a person into believing that a woman in uniform was sexy, the reality was miles away from that fantasy. Everything about a police uniform was utilitarian.

The one exception in Abby's case was her panties; her one true feminine indulgence being sexy underwear. The pair she had on today was a dark blue thong made entirely of lace. Police work was a male-dominated field and she had to wear *something* every day to remind herself that she was a woman.

But right now, she was leaving the panties on not only because they made her feel desirable, but also, because she was sick and tired of waiting. She was here for this incredibly sexy man that she was undeniably attracted to. It was time for her to have the fun she was being accused of.

She crawled onto the bed, straddling Wyatt's body as she moved upward toward him, her one hand catching hold of his shaft. As she leaned forward, pressing her lips against his, she stroked his shaft, feeling his soft skin slide up and down the hardened flesh underneath. Wyatt moaned as her tongue probed his mouth.

She released her hold on him. Wyatt tried to sit up but she pressed him back onto the mattress with the palm on his chest.

"Mine," she growled as she moved so that

she was properly straddling him. Removing her hands from his chest, she reached between her legs and slid the thin line of lace covering her to one side.

Abby actually began to revel in the salacious joy of being the naughty, wanton woman she was accused of being.

Hovering over Wyatt, she stared down at him, her eyes locking onto his. She slid her hand back down between her legs and found Wyatt's shaft. He sucked in a breath and his eyes closed at the pleasure of her hand on him. Abby used her grip on him to get him pointed in the right direction, lowering herself onto him, his head spreading her open, her excitement easing his entrance.

The moment was perfect and her body shuddered as her mind exploded. This was *exactly* what she needed. This was pure ecstasy. Not before this moment had she put into words the desire she'd subconsciously built up for Wyatt. Finally, being this close to this man, quite literally filled with his presence, satisfied a deep-seated longing that she hadn't allowed herself to acknowledge before.

She held herself still as the mental and physical relief cascaded over her. Just as exquisite as the sexual feelings enveloping her was the mental release of all inhibitions. This pure moment of not caring what other people thought did more for her soul than she could've ever imagined.

Her loss of physical control eventually ended. Wyatt had done nothing. He just let her have her moment, something she was immensely grateful for. Her eyes opened and she looked down at him, taking in his pleased expression.

Abby began to move her hips side-to-side, ever so slightly at first. She didn't want to speak but she wanted him to know that it was now time for both of them to enjoy this. He'd been wonderfully understanding; now it was time for her to repay that kindness. And, maybe get a little bit more for herself in the process.

As she moved, he began to lift up into her, matching the subtlety of her movements with his at first and increasing the range of motion and intensity in time with her.

Soon, they were bouncing up and down, lifting and falling in rhythm so that he was meeting her downward motion with his own upward thrust, burying himself in her with each stroke. He filled her perfectly.

She could stand to feel like this forever.

Wyatt grunted with each push upwards. His hands had reached up and grabbed her hips, his fingers digging deliciously into her as he pulled down, using his strength to time their meetings perfectly.

Abby look down at him, mesmerized to find the determination written across his face. His furrowed brow and tightly set jaw drove her wild. The look on his face told her plainly that even though she'd started this, he needed it just as much as she did.

With one final and particularly loud moan of ecstasy, Wyatt's hips thrust upward and he stayed locked in position, his fingers gripping her tightly, pulling her to him. His face was a mask of pure final exertion.

Abby's body reacted instinctively to what was happening and her body joined Wyatt in the wave of pleasure.

All too soon, the moment began to fade. Wyatt's back relaxed, his hips falling to the mattress. It was only then that Abby realized that she'd been holding them in the air. She watched as his eyes reluctantly opened and focused on her face. His smile, spreading slowly, spoke of nothing but pure contentment.

Abby let her own smile spread across her face as she leaned forward, settling herself against his chest. The rise and fall of his breathing combined with the exhaustion of a long and difficult day lulled her into a blissful sleep.

CHAPTER 35

ABBY

S HE WOKE UP with a groan and rolled over, running into something…hard? Her eyes shot open and she came face to face with Wyatt. His eyes fluttered open and he smiled sleepily at her.

"Good morning," he said around a yawn. "Sleep well?"

Oh Lordy. She flopped back onto the bed. She'd actually gone and slept with Wyatt.

Her father was going to *kill* her. She rubbed her eyes with the palms of her hands, groaning. *No, Abby, you're not going to worry about that. You've decided to tell the town of Sawyer to go jump off a cliff, remember?*

She opened up her eyes again and this time, they stayed open. "Yeah, I slept well," she mumbled, finally answering his question.

"You didn't explain much last night," he said, prodding her. "Not that I minded, but do you think you have time to tell me what's going on? You seemed awfully upset, or something, when you showed up."

"Dad. Excuse me, *Sheriff Connelly* pulled me into his office yesterday to tell me that rumors are swirling around town about the two of us. He said that he was talking to me as my boss, but truthfully, as my boss, he legally doesn't have a leg to stand on. I can go hang out with you at Adam's riding arena." She shot him a grin and said, "I probably can't do this," she gestured between them, "legally, but what we have been doing, I was just fine. I don't know – I was getting my ass chewed for something I hadn't even done, and I figured if I was going to get in trouble for sleeping with you, I might as well actually sleep with you, right? If I'm going to do the time, I might as well have done the crime."

He stared at her for a heartbeat, and then began laughing. "That sounds like something I'd say." He grinned at her. "I think I'm a bad influence on you."

"I think you're a *very* bad influence on me," she said, her voice low and sexy.

His eyes darkened. "I think we should discuss just what kind of influence you want me to be over you," he said in a soft voice, stroking her hair away from her face. "Because if I can influence you to come over here and ride me, I think that's the best influence of all."

Memories of the night before raced through Abby's mind and she knew there was no way that she could resist an offer to repeat what had happened. She rolled onto her back and lifted her hips off the bed, finally sliding off the thong panties that had been her only pajamas.

She quickly rolled back toward him, flinging one leg over his body. She scrambled to sit upright, her hands pressing flat against his chest. She could feel his heart pounding against her palms. She slowly rocked her hips forward and backward, grinding herself against him, feeling his excitement growing in time with her own.

Their eyes locked.

"Do you know how beautiful you are?" he asked huskily, his hand moving up her side to grasp a curl of her hair spilling down over her body. "I love every inch of you."

He grasped her waist and swiftly rolled her over onto her back, eliciting a gasp of surprise from her. He grinned down at her naughtily. "I think I need to show you *exactly* what inches of me appreciate you," he said, slipping inside of her. They began moving together, slowly at first and then faster. He closed his eyes, groaning with every thrust.

"Abby, Abby, oh God...*Abby*," and then he was coming inside of her, his hips jerking with each spasm. He felt so amazing inside of her and her back was arching and she was crying out his name, her world coming apart at the seams as she drifted on a sea of happiness.

As she came back down to earth, though, the world came tumbling back down on her head. She'd gone and done it – the one thing her father would never forgive her for.

Twice.

And she had no excuse to offer. All of her self confidence, her willingness to tell the world, or at least her father and Sawyer, to take a hike…it was gone, leaving behind an Abby who felt nothing but panic thrumming through her veins.

CHAPTER 36

WYATT

*a*BBY ABRUPTLY PULLED out of his arms, rolling out of bed without making eye contact, and began throwing her clothes on. "I need to go home and take a shower and get ready for work," she said, staring at the far wall, jerking her clothes on by touch alone. "I'm working the 3 to 11 shift today, so I won't be able to go with you out to Adam's place." She was awkward and fumbling, refusing to meet his eyes, and Wyatt knew that her "Screw the world; I'm going to do what is best for me" attitude had disappeared. She was back to caring, and in a big way.

He sat up in bed, pulling the sheets up around his waist, suddenly not comfortable being naked in front of the woman he'd just made love to, twice. "Thanks for letting me know," he said cooly, trying to act nonchalant. If she didn't care about what they'd shared, neither did he.

Right?

She jerked her head and then left, hurrying down the stairs and out the door. Back to her life. Back to being nothing but friends.

He slammed his hand down on the mattress. "Dammit!" he shouted, throwing himself backwards and staring up at the ceiling. He didn't want to go back to the way things were. He wanted what he had last night, every night. He wanted to wake up to her next to him every morning.

He wanted *her*.

He realized then, that he finally had his answer. For two weeks, they'd "just been friends" because he hadn't known if he could be okay with being childless for the rest of his life. He hadn't known if he could love Abby enough to let go of that dream.

But he realized as he lay there that he knew, better than anyone else, how short life was. How he couldn't take anything for granted.

What if he married someone simply because they had a functioning uterus, but that baby ended up dead, too? Anything could go wrong at any time.

He didn't have any foreshadowing or premonition when Shelly and Sierra left that night to get milk. He didn't know that he'd never see them again. He'd been tired and cranky and out of sorts, and he'd fought with Shelly over that damn milk.

It was a stupid, petty fight, fueled by long, endless days out in the fields, too much caffeine, not enough sleep. It was the kind of fight that a week later, neither of them would've even remembered.

If she'd actually come back home.

She hadn't, of course. His "sure thing" – a gorgeous wife, a beautiful daughter – was gone in an instant.

Why was he turning his back on Abby? Because he wanted another "sure thing"?

Dammit. It wasn't like he had hoards of women, all knocking down his door, wanting to be the wife of a sugar beet farmer, wanting to have seven children in seven years. It wasn't that he thought there was someone else out there for him that he loved more or could love more.

It was the idea of permanently giving up on the idea of having kids. If he closed that door by falling in love with Abby, then he was closing it *forever*.

Falling in love with Abby.

"Wyatt, you're an idiot," he said out loud. Maggie Mae, who'd been sleeping on her blanket in the corner, lifted her head and trotted over, landing a swipe across his face. She wagged her tail, looking at him plaintively. She could tell he was upset, even if she didn't know why.

"Maggie, I'm trying to pretend that whether or not to fall in love with Abby is a choice I'm making. I need to face up to the truth: I've already fallen in love with her. There is no 'maybe' or 'could.' I love her."

Maggie Mae gave him one long lick up the side of his face and he laughed. "Are you voting, too? Do we have a democracy here? You know, if I convince Abby to move in here with me someday, she comes as a package deal. You'll have the cutest crossed-eye cat you've ever seen as a roommate. And I've heard she hates dogs."

Maggie nudged his arm, apparently deciding that if Wyatt was going to lie around and just talk, he ought to be at least petting her while he did it. He moved to scratch her behind the ears, and she closed her eyes in bliss, panting happily. "I can tell you're terrified at the idea of having a cat as a roommate," he said dryly. Maggie ignored him, content to be petted.

He rolled out of bed and Maggie trotted over to the door, ready for the day to begin.

Wyatt figured his dog was smarter than him in a lot of ways, and this was just one of those instances. It was time to start making choices.

Or as Abby put it, it was time to shit, 'cause he didn't want to get off the pot.

CHAPTER 37

ABBY

$\mathcal{D}$AD STORMED DOWN the hallway and slammed into the office. Abby looked at the closed door and back at Officer Morland. "Fun times?" she asked dryly.

He grimaced. "Even for your dad, he's been on one," he said. He pulled off his cap and ran his fingers through his hair, looking like he'd rather be anywhere on earth than right there in that moment. "Listen, I've been meaning to talk to you all day."

He dropped his voice and moved closer to the front desk. "I'm not saying that it's right or wrong, or that you ought to do something different. I just thought I'd let you know that the word went around the office today that your police cruiser was at Wyatt Miller's place all night last night."

A part of her knew that was coming. He wouldn't have come close and talked quietly and stared down at the ground as he did so, if he was informing her that a commendation was coming down the pike.

And if Officer Morland knew, then the chances were good that her dad knew. And if her dad knew…well, that explained why he hadn't talked to her the whole day. She'd rather hoped it was because she'd been so defiant yesterday in his office. She was hoping that he was just still angry over that. Which was a funny thing to hope for, but better that than to be pissed about her spending the night at Wyatt's house.

"Thanks, Morland. I appreciate the head's up."

He nodded, relief washing over him that his duty was done, and he headed outside, off for the day. She, on the other hand, was working the late shift and wouldn't get home until after eleven. Wyatt hadn't exactly let her sleep much the night before, and she had to stifle her yawn. It was going to be a long-ass night.

Chloe came in that evening, after her dad left without saying goodbye. Abby was trying to keep herself awake by filling out reports, and surprising to exactly no one, was failing miserably. Filling out reports would put her to sleep even in the best of times. In fact, she was pretty sure that they should recommend this very activity for people with insomnia.

The glass doors to the jail swung open and in bustled Chloe, packing…food? Abby perked up, the smell of chicken noodle soup wafting towards her nostrils. "Hey!" she said, clearing the corner and hugging Chloe. "What are you doing here?"

Chloe sent her an overly bright smile and said, "We had leftovers today when we closed so I thought I'd bring some over to you."

Abby sent her a questioning glance. "And…?" Because as much as she loved Chloe, this had all the earmarks of a "I'm about to give you really bad news" setup.

"And a couple of people came in today and talked about you and Wyatt." The words came out in a rush, and Chloe asked pleadingly, "Did you *really* spend the night last night at his place?"

Abby dropped her head into her hands, shaking it slowly. "How does this town do it?" she asked rhetorically. "Wyatt lives in the middle of Timbuktu. How would anyone even have seen my cruiser out there?"

"I think it was someone who had to go out there to talk to his farm manager, Jorge. At least, that was the story I was getting."

Abby groaned and opened up the styrofoam carton of soup. If she was going to be tortured by this kind of thing, she could at least do it while eating Betty's homemade soup. She sank into her chair behind the desk, suddenly exhausted beyond words.

"I just wanted to warn you," Chloe said. She didn't look any happier to be the bearer of bad news than Officer Morland had been.

"You know that the people 'round here love nothing more than to gossip. You have to keep your nose clean, or you're going to get run out of town on a rail."

"What if I don't want to keep my nose clean?" Abby asked, staring into the chunks of noodle and broth as she pushed it around with the plastic spoon Chloe had thoughtfully provided.

"You like Wyatt that much?" Chloe's voice was skeptical, and Abby didn't blame her. The Wyatt Chloe knew wouldn't inspire bucking the opinion of every person in town.

But the Wyatt Abby knew, did.

"Yeah, I really do," she said, looking up at Chloe. "I really, really do."

"Well. Okay, then you need to tell everyone else in town to go mind their own business." Chloe sent her a pained grin. "You know I've had that problem myself – single mothers aren't exactly the norm around here, let alone with a child who is half Native American. I got plenty of judgmental looks when I first moved here. I decided that I just didn't care what people thought, and you know what? For the most part, it's worked just fine. There were a couple of times that the more…snobby women in town chose to move sections in the restaurant rather than have me serve them, but somehow, I'm strangely okay with that. Truthfully, I'd rather not be their waitress anyway, if they're going to be like that."

Abby laughed at that. "Good point," she said with a wry smile.

Chloe grew serious again and said, "You need to do what makes *you* happy. But, my word of advice? Stop driving your patrol car out there. If you're not on duty and you're not driving the patrol car out there, no one can legally say a thing to you. They'll say lots of things—" she grinned for a second, "—but let that roll off your back. They're not the kind of people you care about anyway, right?"

Abby stood up and gave her friend a huge hug. "Thank you," she whispered into Chloe's ear.

Chloe squeezed her back tightly and whispered, "I just want you to be happy. Nothing else matters." She pulled away and said a little louder, "I was out and about running errands and wanted to drop that off to you before I headed home again. Call me when you want to chat and catch me up on everything, K?"

Abby nodded and smiled, but let the smile drop as soon as Chloe left. Truth be told, there wasn't much for her to catch her friend up on. She'd stormed over to Wyatt's house, basically demanded that he sleep with her, dragged him to bed, spent the night, pissed the town off (including her father), and then ran out of the house like her ass was on fire as soon as she realized what she'd done.

She'd been so free yesterday. So confident. She was happy to tell this town to go take their gossip and shove it where the sun doesn't shine. She was ready to stand up to her father.

But...that wasn't her. Not really. She was a dutiful daughter who loved her father very much. They didn't always see eye to eye on things, but that was to be expected. It had just been them against the world for so long, she had a hard time remembering back to when it hadn't been that way. As upset as she might get with him, he was still her father. She still had to respect him.

What if Wyatt showed up today and wanted to take you out on a date? A real-honest-to-goodness date like a normal couple? Would you say yes?

She finished the last of her soup staring out the front door, pondering the question. She was pretending, if only to herself, that it was a debate, but truthfully, it wasn't.

She loved her father, but she loved Wyatt more. It was hard for her to imagine defying her father straight up by marrying Wyatt, but that didn't mean that her heart didn't want it. While Wyatt had been busy deciding whether or not he could give up the idea of having children, Abby had been busy falling in love with him.

Which just about made her the dumbest woman on the planet, because Wyatt had never even hinted at feeling the same way towards her. Sure, he'd been willing to get some when she was offering it, virtually throwing it at him, but that just meant he was a guy. It didn't mean he loved her back.

She shouldn't feel this way. She knew that. She should shut her heart off and pull away and walk away and guard herself against the heartache that was coming, because even if for some bizarre reason, Wyatt ended up falling in love with her, could she really defy her father by being together with him?

But not surprisingly, "just walk away" seemed a hell of a lot easier said than done.

CHAPTER 38

WYATT

*D*ONE. It was done. He triumphantly carried the paperwork into the county jail. He realized as he walked in that he probably should've called to make sure Abby would be there before he came over, but he was relieved to spot her behind the counter. She looked up at the sound of the bell over the door ringing and smiled when she saw him.

"Hey Wyatt," she said easily, rising to her feet gracefully. "How are you doing today?"

It'd been three days since she'd run out on him, and they hadn't seen each other once. Hadn't talked. Hell, they hadn't even texted.

He'd been nervous about coming over and dropping the paperwork off; what if she didn't want to see him? But her ready smile seemed to say she wanted to see him as much as he wanted to see her.

He felt himself breathing a little easier.

"Good. I have the paperwork from Adam and from Rhonda. You can look it over, of course, but…I've finished my end of the deal." He handed the paperwork over with a happy smile, and she began shuffling through it, noting the hours worked and the signing off for the counseling appointments.

Finally, she signed at the bottom, made him a photocopy, and said, "Congratulations, Mr. Miller. I will submit your paperwork to Ada County, but as of now, you're in the clear. You are officially off probation. You'll be receiving a confirmation letter in the mail two to three weeks from now."

He grinned, the heavy weight that had been pressing on his chest for months now finally gone. "So I am a free man?" he asked.

"One hundred percent." She looked thrilled for him, almost as thrilled as he felt.

"Good. Then I have a question to ask: Will you be my date this Friday?"

"Your date?" she repeated in a half whisper. She seemed stunned by his question, although how, he couldn't begin to guess. It wasn't like he'd been hiding his feelings from her.

Well, other than the whole "I need to figure out which I love more – you or children" discussion.

Okay, maybe she had every right to look surprised by his question.

"Yes. A date. With me. Out in public. Well, to be more specific, out at my brother's house. Stetson and Jennifer are having a gender reveal party on Friday out at the farm. I want to take you as my date."

Or…

On second thought, as he was telling his plan to Abby, he realized that perhaps she wouldn't be as thrilled about this as he was. He was asking her to go from friends-with-occasional-benefits to dinner-party-with-family. Which even he knew was a Big Deal in the dating world. Not that he was super well-versed in such things, but he'd heard comments through the grapevine once or twice.

He was ratcheting up the level on their relationship by more than a couple of turns of the screwdriver. Or ratchet. He should probably keep his analogies straight.

He was mentally babbling like a buffoon.

Slowly, the smile grew on her face until it was going from ear to ear. "Yes. Yes, I would like that very much, Wyatt."

He nodded once. "Good. See you at 5:30 on Friday? I'll pick you up." He didn't miss the move from "Mr. Miller" to "Wyatt" that she'd just made. He decided that he never liked his first name as much as he did in that moment.

"Okay. Sounds good." She sounded breathy and happy.

He grinned and walked out the door. That was a very fine start to their Friday date, if he did say so himself.

CHAPTER 39

WYATT

HE WALKED INTO Happy Petals, the little bell over the door announcing his arrival. Carla came bustling in from the back, a big smile on her face when she saw him. "Hey Wyatt, long time no see," she said, coming around the counter and giving him a hug. "What're you doing here?"

She'd graduated a couple of years after him – probably in the same class as Abby, actually – but she'd always been friendly to him. She was the huggy sort who loved turquoise and cats, and not necessarily in that order. The shop cat came out with her, twining herself around his legs, and Wyatt leaned down for a moment to pet her, grateful he'd left Maggie Mae at home for once. He really didn't want her chasing a cat around a floral shop, knocking knick-knacks over. That could be a little more fun than he was really up for.

"I...have a date this evening. With a woman." He had no idea why he felt compelled to say that last part. "Abby Connelly," he clarified.

"Oh, I love Abby!" Carla said with a huge smile. Of course she did. She loved everyone, he was pretty sure of it. And the thing was, she was somehow genuine in that. It was the darnedest thing.

"Well, I wanted to bring flowers over when I went to pick her up. Do you have a bouquet I could buy?"

He knew he was in over his head and the water was about to swallow him alive, but thankfully, Carla didn't ask him a single question, like, "What kind of flower?" but instead brought him over to a case.

"Here's what I have on hand. This one

right here is something that I think Abby would like," she said, pointing at a bouquet of pretty flowers. They were lots of different colors and it was a big bouquet.

"Perfect!" he said a little too loudly, but she just smiled at him, pulled the vase out, and rang him up, wishing him luck on his date.

He left, sucking in a huge breath of relief. Flowers were bought; now it was time to shower and shave.

Tonight was going to be awesome.

Dammit.

He turned back around and walked straight back into Carla's shop. "Carla, I forgot – I need a second bouquet of flowers." He couldn't arrive empty-handed to the party tonight, and he wasn't about to go onesie shopping over at Frank's Farm & Feed. He also wasn't about to bring alcohol with him.

She grinned up at him, her eyes twinkling from behind her turquoise glasses. "For Jennifer?" she guessed.

"Damn, you're good," he said admiringly.

"Only because your brother has been

having me deliver flowers once a month to your sister-in-law, to celebrate another month in her pregnancy. Are you taking Abby to the gender reveal party tonight?"

Wyatt tugged on his collar. How did women do it? It was like they were connected to the hive mind or something. "Yeah," he admitted.

"Well good. For Jennifer, your brother has been sending roses and Calla lilies, so I'd suggest that you do something a little less formal since you're a brother-in-law, not her husband."

Wyatt choked. "That's true," he got out. He liked Jennifer and all, and she sure was a step up for his brother, but marry her?

Oh *hell* no. She didn't have all of the curves in the right places like Abby. She was too short. She didn't have Abby's loud laugh. She didn't love horses with every fiber of her being. She didn't have a cross-eyed cat named Jasmine.

No, Jennifer wasn't for him.

It looked like the one he'd just bought for Abby, what with it being all colorful and flowery and shit, but a little bit smaller. "Is that what you had in mind?" she asked.

"Perfect," he said. She really was good at her job.

Which was good for him.

He walked out into the pale winter sunshine that was struggling to come through high, thin clouds, and whistled a nameless tune to himself.

It was going to be a damn good evening.

CHAPTER 40

ABBY

THE DOORBELL RANG, and she hurried over to answer it, smoothing at her dress as she went. She'd spent a lot of time curling her hair and putting on makeup, and was even wearing a dress, which she never did. But a date with Wyatt? Totally worth it.

She opened the door and her heart leapt into her throat. There was Wyatt, holding the most gorgeous bouquet of roses, daisies, and carnations that she'd ever seen. But more than the riot of color in his hands was him.

Handsome him.

Drop-dead gorgeous him.

She stared at him, the door open and letting arctic air into the house, but not giving a damn. Her eyes slowly swept from the brim of his stetson, down over his broad shoulders encased in a thick winter jacket, down to his Wranglers and boots. He'd shaved, and all she wanted to do was explore those cheekbones to see if his skin was as silky smooth as it looked.

He was skimming down over her body too, and he finished his perusal by locking eyes with her, hot with lust. "Hey," he finally got out.

"Hi!" she blurted out, his words spurring her into action. "Sorry, just standing here letting out all the warm air. Let me grab my jacket."

She grabbed her scarf and coat from the hall closet and wrapped herself up in it, then turned back towards him. His arms were still full with the oversized bouquet.

"Oh, the flowers!" she said, blushing and taking them from him. She buried her nose into their depths and breathed in deep. They smelled *amazing*.

She set them down on the end table in her

living room and with one last regretful look back – she hated leaving such beautiful things behind – she walked out into the twilight air. The sun, hiding behind the Goldfork Mountains to the west, still lit up the sky in a hazy way. Pale streaks of gold and pink filtered out. It'd be dark soon.

"Smart thinking on the boots," he said, nodding down towards her footwear. She was wearing knee-high boots that were classy but still ice-and-snow ready. In Sawyer, Idaho, there wasn't much use for high heels.

"Thanks. I thought about wearing my police officer boots, but figured it'd clash with my dress."

He laughed. "I think I would've paid good money to see you in army boots and that beautiful dress."

He thinks my dress is beautiful.

She grinned at him. "You're just going to have to keep your money, then, because I don't plan on doing that any time soon."

He opened up the passenger side door for

her, and helped her get in. "Can you hold these flowers for me?" he asked, handing her a bouquet that'd been on the floor. "They're for Jennifer."

"Sure," she said, happily breathing in the scents from it. It wasn't quite as full or gorgeous as the bouquet he'd bought her, but she knew Jennifer would love them anyway. She'd met Jennifer a few times around town, and had always liked the petite, friendly woman. Although she was from Boise, she didn't turn up her nose at Sawyer, or at least didn't show it if she did.

"So anything exciting happening at the sheriff's office lately?" Wyatt asked as he began pulling out of her circular driveway.

"Not unless you count Mr. Burgemeister's dog treeing Mrs. Willow's cat for the fourteenth time," Abby said dryly. "The fire department had to bring their truck down to get up into the branches, although if you ask me, I think the boys just wanted to get their new shiny toy out and play with it."

The Sawyer Fire Department had just purchased a new fire engine using money from local fundraisers that was matched by the state of Idaho. Abby was pretty sure the fire department would take their new engine out for a joyride around town if they thought they could get away with it.

"Yeah, I heard they're pretty in love with it," Wyatt said with a grin. "Every guy in town wants to drive it, but strangely enough, the fire chief isn't allowing that."

"Strange," Abby said, laughing. They grinned at each other for a moment, sparks flying between them. He leaned over and picked up her hand. Warm and strong, his hand sent sparks through her. She realized after all they'd done together – slept together in his cell at the jail, had sex at his house, kissed at Adam's place – they'd never held hands.

It shouldn't surprise her that they were doing things so backwards. She and Wyatt had never done things in the "proper" order – why would they start now?

"A penny for your thoughts," he said, stroking his thumb over her knuckles.

"I was just thinking that after all we've done, we've never held hands," she said softly, smiling at him.

"There's lots of things we haven't done yet," he said, picking up her hand and bringing it to his mouth. "We haven't had sex outside yet. We haven't—"

"Sex outside?!" she interrupted, laughing. "It's like two degrees out there right now!"

"I didn't say we'd fix that lack in our sex life tonight," he said, grinning. "But if you're up for it, I can think of a couple of other things that we could do tonight that are indoors."

"Oh really?" she asked, breathless. It was funny – she hadn't been running, of course, but it felt like it.

He heard that in her voice; she knew he did because his dropped lower. "I'd been thinking that I hadn't sucked on your toes and given them the attention that they deserved. Did you know that you have the most adorable toes I've ever seen?"

"I do?" This time, her voice ended on a squeak, and he began laughing.

"As a matter of fact, you do," he said. His voice was deep and rumbling and she felt it all the way down to the aforementioned toes.

"Oh," she got out. They finally arrived at the Miller farm, saving her from making any further nonsensical replies.

Which she was grateful for, on one hand, but it also meant that he wasn't saying anything that would inspire nonsensical replies. Which she wasn't quite as grateful about.

Wyatt helped her out of the truck and, tucking her arm into his, they made their way up the sidewalk. Before they reached the front door, though, it swung wide open.

"Hello!" Declan said, the bright welcoming light streaming out from behind him. He and Wyatt shook hands, and then Declan gave her a warm hug. "How are you? I'm so glad you came."

They chatted as they removed coats and then moved through the house to the crowded kitchen, where Carmelita was in full form, whipping up what appeared to be enchiladas, homemade chips and salsa, and enough finger foods to feed a small army. Abby smiled at the older lady. She hadn't spent a lot of time around her, but knew she was a magician in the kitchen, and that she loved Stetson like her own.

Especially that second fact endeared her to Abby. None of the Miller boys had had it easy growing up, but she figured Stetson losing his mom when he was only twelve had it the worst of all.

"Hi!" Jennifer came around the corner, a huge smile on her face, her belly bulging out in front of her like she'd swallowed a volleyball for breakfast. On such a petite woman, the bump was even more noticeable. Abby figured she had to be the most adorable pregnant woman she'd ever laid eyes on. "Welcome to this madhouse!"

Abby held the flowers out to her and Jennifer took them with a hug and a kiss on the cheek. "And welcome to the family," she whispered into her ear.

Abby pulled back, blushing. Jennifer just buried her face in the flowers, smelling them and smiling. "I don't mean to freak you out," she whispered conspiratorially, "but I have it from the best source out there that the last person Wyatt brought home to meet the family was Shelly."

Abby blushed harder. "We're not exactly to that point yet," she whispered back.

"The Miller boys move fast," Jennifer said confidently. "If they like something they see, they don't sit around and wait. They jump on it."

Abby laughed hard at that one. The rumor around town was, Stetson had only known Jennifer for a couple of weeks before he'd proposed to her. No, the Miller boys didn't exactly let the grass grow under their feet.

"Come on, let me find a jar to put this bouquet into." Jennifer grabbed her by the arm and led her out of the kitchen and down the hallway. "It's best to leave Carmelita alone right now," she said in a low voice. "She's been working on this party for the last two weeks and at this point, I think staying in the kitchen for more than five minutes at a time is risking death by butcher knife."

Abby threw back her head and laughed.

Yeah, spending time with the Miller family wasn't going to be hard to do at all.

CHAPTER 41

WYATT

IT SEEMED LIKE AS SOON AS they arrived, Abby was being whisked off by Jennifer to go do…something. He hadn't really caught what, but he figured that it was good to leave them to it. He could totally mix and mingle with the fine citizens of Long Valley on his own.

He didn't exactly look forward to it, but he could do it.

"Want a lemonade or something?" Declan asked, appearing suddenly at his elbow.

Declan. He latched onto him. Here was someone he could hang out with and talk to. "Sure," he said with an overly bright smile.

"Be right back," Declan said, disappearing into the crowd.

Dammit. He didn't exactly want to be left behind, but he wasn't sure what else to do at that point. He also didn't want to follow his younger brother around like a lost puppy dog.

He glanced around the living room. The chief of police for the city, the head librarian, even the clerk from the Shop 'N Go, were all talking and milling around. When did Stetson become friends with all of these people? Jennifer must've gotten him out of his shell. She was good for him in more ways than one.

His brother showed up at his elbow again, but it was Stetson this time, not Declan. "Hey," Stetson said. "Declan said this is for you." He handed Wyatt a lemonade in a green Solo cup.

"Thanks." He took a sip, enjoying the tart and sweet mixed together.

They just stood there and watched the crowd for a moment. Finally, Wyatt offered up, "Quite the shindig you have going on here."

"Yup. Shoulda seen Carmelita. She's been going nuts the last two weeks. I've never seen her cook so many dishes in all my life."

They fell silent again, the country music twanging under the current of laughter and talk flowing through the room.

"Mom and Dad would be real happy if they could see this," Wyatt finally said.

Stetson nodded real slowly. "I've been thinking about them a lot lately. I'm real sorry Mom isn't going to be able to meet this grandchild. Or Jennifer."

"Yeah. She would've loved it."

It was quiet again between them, but for the first time in…years, perhaps, Wyatt wasn't sure – it wasn't a tense silence. Seeing Stetson here, taking care of their family home, starting a family of his own…Wyatt kept waiting for the green-eyed monster to flare up inside of him. For him to feel anger that once again, Stetson was being handed a wife and child without even having to try, but instead, he just felt pleasant. Warm. Relaxed.

Rhonda was right…the only thing I can control is my reaction.

It was a stunning thought, to see proof of it in front of him.

"Thanks for coming," Stetson finally said, clapping Wyatt on the back.

"Dinner is ready," Carmelita called out, and the room instantly hushed. Wyatt was pretty sure he wasn't the only one in attendance whose mouth was watering. "You can start at that end and work your way through the line this way," she said, pointing to the dining room table practically groaning underneath the weight of the food.

Stetson looked around. "I better find my wife," he said. "She wouldn't want to miss this." He disappeared up the stairs. Wyatt looked around for Abby. Was she still with Jennifer? He saw Luke Nash, a friend of Stetson's, with his arm around some pretty lady who he assumed was Bonnie. He'd heard from Declan that while they'd been bunked up at the jail on Christmas Eve, Luke had been here on the farm, along with Bonnie, and they'd fallen in love in the middle of that blizzard.

Abby and I weren't the only ones to find each other during that blizzard.

Finally, he spotted Abby and worked his way over to her. He slipped his arm around her waist and gave her a peck on the cheek.

"Oh hi!" she said, turning a delicious shade of pink. He instantly decided to try to make her turn that color every day. She was gorgeous when she was flushed. She was gorgeous all the time, really. Even with her service belt on and her thick black officer boots and her hair pulled back in a bun, she took his breath away.

So with her hair down and curled and a flowing dress on that emphasized her tits and spiky boots that emphasized her ass? He wasn't entirely sure how to breathe around her.

After they grabbed their plates of food, though, Abby got pulled away by Jennifer to meet Bonnie, and Wyatt was left by himself with his plate of food.

He looked around the crowded living room,

and finally decided to step outside for a moment for a quick breather. It was crowded and a little too warm and there were a little too many people in there. He'd never exactly been the social one in a group, but he'd become even more withdrawn, even happier to be by himself, since spending quality time down at the county jail.

He walked out the back door and onto the back porch. Carmelita and Jennifer had even strung lights along the edge of the porch, alternating blue and pink light bulbs. They weren't going to give the gender away even here. He took a deep breath of the freezing cold air, almost enjoying the burn in his lungs. At least he was able to breathe out here.

The door opened and closed behind him and he turned, a smile on his face. Abby probably saw him slip outside and was wondering what was—

It wasn't Abby. "What are you guys doing here?" he asked, staring at the three men coming out of the house.

"What? You think we're not good enough

to be invited to your brother's party?" Jack sneered.

"Nope. I don't."

He also couldn't believe that Stetson would invite them. Jack and his two sidekicks, Larry and Moe as Wyatt had mentally christened them years ago, had been employees of Sheriff Connelly...right up until Wyatt had bought the farm off the auction block and fired them.

It was the first thing he'd done when he'd taken it over. He'd never understood why the sheriff had held onto them like he had; they were the town drunks and they weren't the nice kind. They got into more fistfights than he did, and that was saying something.

"Well, maybe you don't know your brother like you think you do," Moe – or was it Larry? – taunted him. "You two aren't exactly close."

"Either way, you need to get out of my face," Wyatt growled. The three men were advancing on him, ganging up on him, and he started to feel claustrophobic again. Jack jostled against him, and Wyatt tightened his grip around his lemonade. *You can't choose what they do, only what your reaction is to them.*

He took a deep breath and a sip of his lemonade, letting the sour-sweet liquid slide down his throat. "Listen, you guys, I don't want to start something, okay? Not here, not tonight."

"What if *we* do?" Jack said, taunting him, so close Wyatt could smell his tobacco-ridden breath. "You're a piece of shit who was so lazy, you couldn't be bothered to go out for milk. Killed your own wife and daughter. What if we think scum like you should be cleaned off the face of the planet?"

Like a tidal wave roaring over his head, Wyatt's vision went red.

CHAPTER 42

ABBY

FOR WHAT SEEMED LIKE the hundredth time, Abby looked around the crowded house, trying to find Wyatt. He'd been right there, and then…well, she wasn't quite sure what'd happened, actually. Everyone seemed to want to either talk to him or her tonight, and for being on their very first official date, they hadn't spent but ten minutes around each other.

Right then, Stetson clinked his fork against a beer bottle. "I've been informed by my lovely wife that it's time to cut the cake," he said. "As you all know, Jennifer is due in April and has spent the last two weeks taunting me by telling me that she knows whether or not we're having a girl or a boy, but refuses to share the information with me." A small ripple of laughter went through the audience, and Abby grinned too.

Jennifer had told her earlier that Stetson had refused to know, wanting to hear it along with everyone else, but apparently that didn't keep him from teasing her. She stuck her tongue out at him, which caused an even louder wave of laughter to run through the room.

Abby craned her neck. Where was Wyatt? He was missing the big reveal.

She hadn't said anything all evening – not that she had much of a chance *to* say anything to him – but she was worried about how he was going to take this party. After all, it was a celebration for his younger brother, who Wyatt didn't exactly get along with, getting the one thing that Wyatt wanted more in the world than anything: Children.

What if he was hiding in a room somewhere, trying to keep from punching holes in the wall because he was frustrated? He'd wanted to go to this party; he'd asked her to come along with. Maybe the idea of attending was okay, but actually being here was too much? Maybe it was weirding him out.

Abby's attention was jerked back to the front of the room when people began chanting, "Cut it, cut it, cut it." Stetson and Jennifer were holding a knife together, hovering over a giant cake from the Muffin Man. It made Abby grin – they looked just like a couple would on their wedding day. The knife entered the cake, once, twice, and then Stetson was pulling out the wedge with his bare hands.

"A boy!" he hollered, showing the blue cake to the cheering, laughing crowd. He shoved it into his mouth as everyone swarmed to give their congratulations to the couple.

"You better hope he takes after your wife in looks," was what more than one teasing friend made sure to tell Stetson. Abby hid her grin. Stetson was sure a handsome guy...but he was no Wyatt.

Speaking of, where on earth had he gone?

She decided to make a systematic search of the house, checking each room, even knocking on the bathrooms, which was inexcusably rude but she didn't have a choice. She was genuinely starting to get worried at this point, so good manners be damned.

Well, he wasn't in the house, which meant…he'd gone outside? It was freezing cold and dark out there. Why on God's green earth would he go out there? She worked her way through the crowds and out the backdoor. Maybe he just needed a breath of fresh air and had let time slip away—

Which was when she saw him. Sitting on a bench, holding his hand up to his face. She got closer, squinting in the shifting shadows from the house and the pale moon overhead.

"Helwhoa," he slurred, through a mouth full of broken teeth and blood. Even in the uncertain light, she could tell he was developing a black eye. Maybe two.

She heard a stick crack in the distance and her head shot up. There were three figures melting into the forest. Her first instinct was to run to Wyatt's side and check over his injuries, but her police training kicked in. She scanned the scene.

There were open beer bottles and cans all over the back deck. The snow on the deck was scuffled and trampled, and there were spots of blood everywhere.

Wyatt had come out here to get drunk, and then picked a fight with some guys once he was nice and rummy?

"Was you doing?" he slurred, looking up at her through his better eye.

He was drunk.

Wyatt Miller, the very last person on earth who should ever touch alcohol, had gotten smashing drunk. *And* got in a fight. She'd been right to worry – Stetson's news had been too much for him after all. He'd been doing so good…

And then he broke.

He broke and went right back to what he'd always done – fixed his problems with his fists. Although she had to hand it to him: Getting drunk was a new one for him. If he was going to go down, he obviously was going to go down in flames.

She felt anger sweep over her — anger and frustration and rage and she realized she was livid. She wasn't just angry; no, that was too benign. She was *livid*. She was shaking.

She was going to kill him.

She stalked over to him and jerked him to his feet. He yelped in pain and she figured he'd hurt his ribs somewhere along the way. *Good. He deserves pain. Out of all of the stupid stunts to pull in the world, this was the kicker.*

She left her purse inside; she'd go back and get it later. Right now, she was going to drag Wyatt's sorry ass out to the truck.

"You damn idiot," she ground out as she dragged him along. He was stumbling in the semi-darkness, and she didn't even care.

"Where's we going?" he mumbled.

"To jail. You couldn't even make it a damn week, could you? You just finished probation and *bam!* Right back into jail you're going to go." She opened up the passenger side of the truck and shoved him in, slamming the door behind him. She stalked around to the driver's side and pulled his keys out of the door pocket where he'd dropped them earlier and shoved them into the ignition, bringing the diesel engine roaring to life.

"And this time!" she yelled, gunning the engine and weaving through the parked cars to get back to the main driveway, "I hope they lock you up and throw away the key! You're drunk, Wyatt, damn drunk! I can smell it coming off you in waves. After everything that happened, you go and get drunk at your *brother's party?*"

They bounced along the rutted dirt road until she spotted the stop sign ahead, gleaming in the darkness. She made a quick check both ways and then ran the stop sign. No one was coming, and at that point, she couldn't begin to make herself give a damn. She roared down the highway towards Sawyer. Wyatt's head was lolling around as he mumbled to himself but she didn't bother asking him to repeat himself louder. Whatever he had to say, he could say it to a judge.

She was sick of defending him. Not when he was going to take that trust and throw it away like this.

The dim lights of Sawyer began to show between the trees, and then Main Street burst into view as she came around the corner. She wished she was in her police cruiser and could flip on the lights and just bust through town, but she'd stupidly been on a *date* with Wyatt Miller and so she wasn't driving her cruiser and she didn't have handcuffs on her, although the idea of snapping them around his wrists just then sounded wonderfully appealing.

She pulled up right outside of the courthouse, the massive truck taking up three spaces because of her shitastic parking job. She couldn't bring herself to care about that either. She yanked the keys from the ignition and stalked around to the passenger side door, pulled it open and practically rolled Wyatt out of the truck.

Just how drunk was he? He had to have been doing shots outside. Had he carried a flask of whisky in with him without her noticing? Her anger burned hotter as she half dragged, half pulled him into the jail. Officer Rios' head shot up at her entrance, and his eyes grew wide.

"What the hell?" he asked, bounding around the edge of the desk to stop in front of them. He looked back and forth between Abby in her civilian clothes and Wyatt in his dressy shirt, and then up to his bloodied and swollen face.

"Apparently, this is how Wyatt celebrates his brother having his first child," Abby ground out. For the first time since it all started, she felt tears prick the edges of her eyes. She'd had so much hope…and it was all gone.

Wiped out in a single night.

"Book him on drunken and disorderly conduct," she said, the ice closing around her heart in stark contrast to the heat of the tears threatening to spill down her cheeks. She jerked her arm away from him, half hoping he'd collapse to the floor of the jail office, but he managed to stay on his feet, wavering around, a half smile curling his lips. He looked for all the world like he was *enjoying* this.

"Is there an officer on patrol?" she barked.

"Yeah, Morland."

"Can you radio him? I need a ride home since this jackass was my ride to the party. His truck is parked outside; it'll probably have to be moved to a more…appropriate location." Considering she was practically blocking the entrance to the jail with her stellar parking job, but she just couldn't bring herself to care about that at the moment.

Nodding, Rios radioed Morland with one hand as he wrapped his arm around the waist of Wyatt, directing him back to the drunk tank – the cell where they put the drunks to sleep off the alcohol.

Abby tossed Wyatt's keys onto the desk and went outside to wait in the cold and the dark for her ride, the light wind piercing her dress, and even as her teeth chattered from the cold, hot tears blazed their way in an endless trail down her cheeks.

CHAPTER 43

WYATT

HE SWAM TO THE SURFACE, his head throbbing from the pain. There was light, and he wanted it to go away. He wanted everything to go away. Why was there so much light? He groaned.

"You awake?" he heard a deep voice ask.

He tried to open his eyes but there was pain and light and he closed them tight again, with a louder groan this time. "Where…where am I?" he rasped.

"The Long Valley Jail," the voice said, a hint of amusement in it. "I would've thought you'd had enough of this place, but here you are, back again."

"Why?" he whispered. His throat was parched and it was hard for him to get any sound out, but he had to know. He had to figure this out. Something was wrong. Really wrong. He peeked one eye open, and Officer Rios' face swam into view.

"I'm gonna go get the sheriff," the officer said, blatantly avoiding Wyatt's question. "He told me to tell him as soon as you were awake."

"Water," Wyatt croaked. If he was going to have to face the sheriff, he at least wanted to be able to talk. It wasn't a fair fight otherwise. The officer nodded and quickly returned with a water bottle. Room temperature, but Wyatt didn't even care.

After dribbling some into his mouth, he slowly sat upright, trying to keep the world from spinning out of control. It went this way and that on him, and he reached up, cradling his head in his hands. He slowly scanned the holding tank, and spotted a toilet in the corner.

Good. He might need to upchuck the contents of his stomach at any moment.

Why did he feel like this? He was so confused. He tried to think back to what he last remembered. Picking up Abby from her house, and petting Jasmine while he was there. Then driving to Stetson's house. It was the big party. He tried to remember the cake cutting – the big reveal of whether they were having a girl or boy, but it was a dark abyss. Nothing. Why couldn't he remember them cutting the cake? That was the whole point of the party. Stetson was never going to forgive him for forgetting one of the biggest moments of his life.

Whatever happened, it had to be why he felt like he'd been run over by a one-ton truck. He didn't get to feeling this way by going out and having a fine time at his brother's baby shower, for hell's sake. Especially not one where all he'd been drinking was lemonade.

He sniffed, gingerly at first and then deep breaths.

He sure as hell didn't smell like he'd been drinking lemonade. He smelled like a brewery.

Which officially made no sense whatsoever. He hadn't touched alcohol since the night Shelly and Sierra had died. He couldn't. Not after all it took away from him. It didn't bother him when others drank around him – unless they were trying to get behind the wheel of a car, of course – but for him? Never.

It sure smelled like he had, though.

The sheriff came through the door separating the front office area from the jail cells and walked down the cell block, his boots loud on the concrete floor. Wyatt struggled to his feet. Whatever he'd done, he wanted to face the sheriff standing up like a man.

He expected the sheriff to bark at him through the bars but instead he pulled his keys from his belt and unlocked the cell. He opened the door wide and stood in it, leaning against the metal frame casually, crossing one foot over the other. But his shoulders and jaw...no matter how casual he was trying to appear, he wasn't feeling it at all.

In fact, Wyatt would guess he was right on

the edge of total breakdown. Or panic. Or something.

The sheriff cleared his throat. "I suppose I owe you an apology," he said gruffly.

Wyatt stared at him. He felt like he'd fallen down the rabbit hole. He couldn't have been more surprised if the sheriff had walked in and announced that he was actually a transvestite.

"Wh-what?" he finally got out.

"My momma woulda had my hide for that," the sheriff continued, ignoring Wyatt's stuttering. "She sure hated it when people said it like that. So let me try it again. Wyatt, I am apologizing for my behavior in the past. And, probably for what I'll do in the future."

"Wh-what?" he repeated. Not exactly his finest hour, but he was so far away from being able to make heads or tails of the situation, the sheriff might as well have started talking in Chinese. He would understand just as much.

"Last night, you had the misfortune of running into three of my old employees."

Jack, Moe, and Larry. The memory was there, clear as day, as if he should've been able to remember it all along. They'd been outside when he'd gone out to get a breath of fresh air. How could he have forgotten that?

"My daughter dragged you back here last night and dropped you off with some choice words about you getting drunk. Officer Rios booked you, and as a matter of course, had you breathe into a breathalyzer. Do you remember any of this?"

Wyatt shook his head. For some reason, he couldn't remember past meeting the three Stooges out on the back deck. Why was it a big blank?

"You blew a zero."

"Zero?" Wyatt repeated. He really wished he could stop parroting every word the sheriff was saying, but he needed the world to start making sense. Any minute now…

"You hadn't touched a drop. Which made Rios a might bit suspicious, considering you smelled like you'd taken a bath in alcohol and you were waving around on your feet like you'd just finished a chugging contest at a frat party. So we had you tested for the date rape drug."

"I got raped?" Wyatt's voice broke halfway through the question and he stared in horror at the sheriff.

"No, no, that's just the name most people know it by. We had the doctor stop by – you have some broken teeth that'll require some dental work, and some bruises to your ribs, oh and a cut over your eye, but your ass was untouched.

"No, you got framed. My three former employees, may they rot in hell, were picked up by Officer Morland after he dropped Abby off at home. They'd made their way down to O'Malley's and had begun bragging about what they did to pretty much anyone within earshot. They crashed the party, dropped the drug in your drink, and then after they kicked the ever livin' hell outta you, they poured some beers on ya. They figured you'd get arrested for fighting in public again, and this time, with the charges of drinking on top of it, well, that'd just about finish your time here in Sawyer."

Wyatt sank back down to the cot and stared up at the sheriff. "Why? How?"

"They're dumbasses, so it didn't take much to break 'em. I basically looked at them and told 'em to start talking, and it all came out. You fired them when you bought my farm."

The change in topic midway through his statement seemed to make sense to the sheriff, at least, and he paused, waiting for Wyatt to speak. Finally, Wyatt said slowly, "Yeah, I did. I knew they were troublemakers and I didn't want them on the place. It's the first thing I did when I bought it." He couldn't figure out what that had to do with anything and just stared at the sheriff, hoping he'd continue his story.

"Well, I guess they've been harboring a grudge ever since. They had a hard time finding a job because you wouldn't give them a recommendation; I figure their reputation also proceeded them and no one with a half a brain would choose to bring them on, but they're pinning it all on you. Jack lost his house; the bank repo'd it. I think one of the others had his wife divorce him because he wasn't holding down a steady job."

He heaved a huge sigh, running his hands

through his salt-and-pepper hair. "Truth is, I should've fired 'em myself. I was struggling from losing my wife, and then the rains weren't coming and I knew I was going to lose my farm, and I just couldn't get myself to care enough to fire 'em. It was the last thing on my mind, although they were certainly not stellar employees for me. In your shoes, I would've done the same thing as you."

"So…they've been hating me ever since because I fired them? And they tried to make me look bad at my brother's party last night?" Wyatt felt about seven miles thick, but even through the fog, things were starting to come together.

"Yeah, that's the long and short of it. I have them en route to Ada County. Being my former employees and all and the fact that we're not really meant to be a long-term jail here, I'm sending 'em over there." He heaved a big sigh. "I should've done that with you. We're not big enough to justify a jail being staffed full-time year-round. I just…didn't want to send you elsewhere."

Wyatt nodded slowly, trying to keep his head from bobbing off into Pain Land. He figured if the sheriff was going to spend this much time apologizing to him, Wyatt could give his own apology another shot.

"Speaking of," he said gruffly, and then cleared his throat. He liked apologizing about as much as the sheriff did, he figured. Maybe even less. "When I bought your farm and went down to O'Malley's to celebrate, I wasn't talking about you when I said that I'll show him how to run a farm. I was talking about my dad. He'd been letting Stetson do whatever he wanted, whenever he wanted, for years. We'd been knocking heads over the farm for a long time, and I finally had my chance to show him how a *real* farm was run. That comment had nothing to do with you."

"I can see that," the sheriff said, nodding his head slowly. "Thanks for letting me know."

And just like that, the topic was dropped.

"So, am I free to go?" Wyatt asked.

"Yup. We'll keep you updated on how the case goes with the numbnuts. Are you feeling well enough to drive home, or should I have one of our officers take you there?"

Wyatt stood and took a few exploratory steps forward to see how his head responded. "I think I'm all right to drive," he said. "I'll just take it slow."

"Sure, sure," the sheriff said, and they headed up to the front together.

CHAPTER 44

ABBY

BBY PULLED INTO her parking spot at the courthouse, staring out at the frozen, dead landscaping in front of her. Bushes that were nothing but a skeleton of branches, piles of brown, crusty snow littered with dead leaves.

All rather what her heart felt like, actually. Dead and brown and frozen.

Which felt awfully dramatic, but also damn true. Blinking twice, she realized that she was still in her car. She should get out, and you know, go to work or something. She heaved a sigh and clambered out of her car.

Today was going to be awful, no doubt about it. Her father was going to pull her into his office and tell her that this was *exactly* what he knew was going to happen, and how dare she go to this party with Wyatt; didn't she know what kind of a guy he was?

Something he so conveniently proved yet again.

She trudged towards the door of the jail. One foot, the other foot. She slipped inside quietly, the bell jingling overhead alerting everyone to her presence anyway. *Dammit.*

"Abby, in my office please!" her father barked, and then disappeared down the hallway.

That didn't take long.

Well, it was probably best to just get it over with and move on with her life. She wondered if her father was going to fire her. She saw Officer Rios looking at her as she passed him at the desk, but she couldn't bring herself to look at him. She didn't want to see the pity in his eyes as she was raked over the coals...or pitched out on her ear.

She closed the door behind her without even being asked. This was one conversation she didn't want anyone to overhear. She stared sightlessly at the far wall, her eyes burning from the endless tears that had watered her pillow last night. Jasmine hadn't left her side once, snuggling against her and occasionally licking the tears away as the clock ticked on. If Abby'd fallen asleep at some point, she couldn't recall it.

"Abby, I am apologizing."

Abby snapped her head to stare at her father in shock, and the world swam a little with the suddenness of the movement. *Surely* he hadn't said what she thought he said. Maybe she'd gone from depressed to delusional. Her father *never* apologized for anything.

Ever.

"Don't give me that look," he said with a grim chuckle. "This is my second apology in as many hours, and I'm enjoying it about as much as you might expect."

Her mouth opened and closed, but no words came out. There were no words left. Her father had apologized twice in one day? To whom? She felt a little faint.

"Wyatt was set up last night at his brother's party. He was slipped a date rape drug and then those three yahoos who used to be my employees took their time beating him up and pouring beers all over him to make him look like he'd been drinking up a storm. Luckily for Wyatt, they were too stupid to think to make him drink anything, so he blew a zero last night when Rios was trying to book him. Then they were even more dumb as to go down to O'Malley's and get so blitzed, they thought bragging about what they'd done to anyone within earshot was a damn good idea.

"After Morland dropped you off last night, Steve called from the bar and told him what those idiots were saying. He arrested them and brought them here. I questioned them and they broke after I heavily interrogated them by asking them, 'What happened last night?' Hardened criminals we have going on here."

Abby felt the giggle start low within her and then begin to bubble up until it burst out. She laughed and laughed, leaning against the chair to support herself as her legs grew weak. Her father just watched her and smiled, giving her the time to work through the info he'd just dumped on her head.

"That makes so much more sense," she finally got out. "I'd never seen Wyatt touch alcohol, so last night, to be so drunk...it confused me, but not enough to make me stop and ask why.

"Oh no, Dad..." She straightened up and looked at him with horror. "He has to hate me right now, for believing the worst of him, when he hadn't done a damn thing to deserve it."

"That brings me to part two of our little discussion," her dad continued, as if he hadn't heard her. She gulped. *Now* he was going to yell at her for attending the party last night with Wyatt. She *knew* the other shoe would drop. "You've got the rest of the day off. With pay. You and Wyatt need to go pull your heads out of your asses and talk to each other. I'm hereby ordering you off the courthouse property, with a strongly worded suggestion to go find Wyatt and talk to him."

Now she really was sure she was delusional. "You want me to go work things out with Wyatt?" she asked, feeling about ten feet thick. Because that was *surely* not what he'd meant to say.

Surely.

"Wyatt and I had our chat this morning and cleared the air between us. I'm just saying that you need to go do that with him yourself. Now whether you end up doing…whatever, is up to you two." His cheeks turned just a little pink and he looked distinctly uncomfortable. "You two are adults and can do as you like. I'm just telling you that you need to go *talk* to him." He put just a smidge bit of emphasis on the word *talk* and Abby swallowed the giggles threatening to erupt out of her again.

She hadn't been asking if she ought to go bang Wyatt, but obviously that's what her father thought she'd meant, and now…well, the topic was just too weird by half. She was going to leave before her father felt compelled to have

The Talk with her. Not that she could get pregnant, of course, but STDs…

She realized she was still just standing there in her father's office. "Leaving!" she blurted out and did an about face to head to the door.

It was time to *talk* to Wyatt Miller, and, God willing, a whole lot more.

CHAPTER 45

WYATT

E WAS LYING on the couch with an ice pack over his eyes, trying not to let the world whirl around him too much, when he heard the crunch of tires on gravel. For a man who didn't normally receive many visitors, he sure was getting a lot of them lately. He swung his feet over and sat up with a groan. It was probably Stetson or Declan, here to chew him out for leaving the party early. He'd meant to call and apologize to Stetson and relay what happened, but hadn't honestly felt up to it.

Well, whether he felt up to it or not, it was

happening now. He forced himself to his feet and shuffled over to the front door. At least he'd taken a shower when he got home, so he didn't smell like he fell into a vat of beer anymore. He wasn't sure if Stetson would let him talk long enough to explain *that* smell away.

He opened the door just as Abby was raising her hand to knock. They both froze, staring at each other.

"Abby?" he finally said. That couldn't be right. He had to still be dreaming. He closed his eyes, counted to three, and opened them again. She was still standing there.

"Pinch me!" he said impulsively, holding out his arm.

She shot him a look that clearly questioned his sanity, but did so anyway.

"Ow!" he yelped, yanking his arm back.

He was awake all right.

He stood back and held the door open for her. "Come on in," he said graciously, as if that whole exchange had not just happened. Perhaps if he ignored it, she would too. Sending him a sideways glance that told him she had not in fact contracted amnesia in the last 30 seconds, she walked past him and into the house.

Which was when he first noticed that she wasn't wearing her uniform, or her Wranglers and a pearl-snap western shirt. She was wearing slacks that hugged her curves just right and a low-cut blue blouse that hugged and showed off her upper curves just right.

He struggled to keep his eyes on her face, her breasts acting like a magnet for his eyeballs. She looked damn amazing, with makeup and hair curled and…he breathed in deep… lemons. How was it that she always smelled like lemons?

"We need to talk," she finally said into the silence. "Believe it or not, my father ordered me over here."

"Your dad is playing matchmaker?" Wyatt asked incredulously.

"Believe me, I think it was just as shocking to me." She sent him a grin. "We veered dangerously close to the birds and the bees territory today." She waved her hand in the air dismissively. "Never mind that. I'm here to apologize to you about last night. I should've realized that something was going on because you were just acting so out of character, but then again, you'd been in a massive fight and your face was banged up, so that part kinda felt pretty in character." She let out a short laugh. "I should've known that something was going on, though."

She took a deep breath and looked him straight in the eye, growing completely serious. "I'm sorry for believing the worst in you. I'm sorry for thinking that you hadn't changed."

He walked over to her and scooped her hands up into his. "Abby, you had every reason to think what you did. Hell, this past summer, I got into a fistfight with Stetson over him almost losing the Miller Family Farm. I rearranged a guy's face and he ended up in the hospital. I'm not saying that both of them didn't deserve exactly what happened," he gave her a sorry-not-sorry grin, "but I am saying that I'm not exactly known for having Mother Theresa qualities. You can call me many things, but peacemaker ain't one of them."

He raised her hands to his mouth and kissed them. "I've spent years punching my way through every situation. I consider a conversation with Stetson that doesn't end in a fistfight to be a win. Being around you and Adam and the kids and the counselor...it's showing me that punching people isn't always necessary. I will admit, though, that if I see those three scumbags again, I may or may not be tempted to break my vow of peace."

Her eyes, watching his every movement with kindness and passion, lit up with laughter at that comment. "I'd be tempted to hold 'em down for you," she admitted. "If there was ever a group of people deserving a beat down by you, it's those three. I'm just glad they're as dumb as they are mean. If they'd forced you to drink a couple of shots of whisky or something, and if they'd managed to keep their mouths shut instead of getting wasted down at O'Malley's and bragging to anyone who'd stop long

enough to listen, I doubt we would've ever figured it out."

"Truth be told, the old Wyatt deserved to
have that believed about him. I've done a lot of
shitty things in my life. I'm not about to pretend
that I don't deserve to have people question my
motives and my actions. But you're showing me
a better way, and...I like it. I like not having a
ball of anger knotting up my stomach all the
time. Strange but true." They laughed quietly
together at that, and then it struck him. "Hey, I
missed it – am I getting a niece or a nephew?"

"A nephew," Abby said, a huge grin on her
face. "The interior of the cake was blue. I
thought Stetson was gonna pick Jennifer up
and carry her around, he was so happy. The
thing is, I think he would've been just that
happy if the cake was pink. He's thrilled to
death about this baby. And Carmelita too. I
know you guys miss your parents something
fierce, but this baby is lucky to have a grandma
like Carmelita around."

Wyatt nodded. "I was too old for her to step

into the role of mother when Mom passed, but Stetson was just a kid – only twelve – and I know they became really close after that. I was lucky to have my mom around until I was 18. She was such a wonderful lady – she would've loved you."

Love.

It was time. He pulled in a deep breath. "Abby Connelly, I love you. I love you with all of my heart and soul. A part of me will always love and miss Shelly and Sierra, but they are my past. You are my future. It doesn't matter to me that you can't have kids. Sure, I'd love a little Abby running around, but more impor-tant than some hypothetical child is being with *you*. That's what matters in this world, and it's actually Shelly and Sierra who taught me that. I thought I had forever with them. I thought…" His voice broke, and he cleared it, trying to move past the lump in his throat. "I was wrong about them. I don't want to be wrong about you. I love you—"

She pressed her lips against him then, cut-ting him off, and he felt moisture on his hands that were cupping her face and he knew she was crying but she was kissing him and tugging at his shirt and he couldn't help kissing her back, tears be damned. She could be crying tears of happiness for all he knew. Right then, all he wanted was to show her how much he loved her, with his tongue and his body and his hands.

He scooped her up into his arms and began carrying her up the stairs. "What?!" she shrieked when he picked her up. "Wyatt, you're going to hurt yourself!"

"Don't you worry about me," he said with a huge grin down at her. "I'm just fine. Not as fine as you're going to be in just a couple of minutes here, of course."

She grinned back up at him, and he took the stairs two at a time, the pain that had been wracking his body just a half hour before mysteriously gone.

Abby had just that kind of effect on him.

Once they made it to the bedroom, he slowly allowed her to slide down his body, the ache of his cock growing stronger by the moment. She spun around and flung herself against him, her hands starting to work on the buttons of his shirt. His hands slid down her back, enjoying the feel of her beneath his fingertips.

She managed to unfasten the last button just as his hands came to rest on the curve of her ass, and she tugged at it, the fabric reluctantly pulling free of his Wranglers.

She placed her hands on his chest. The coolness of her soft hands felt wonderful against his skin. The trail left by her touch excited him, reminding him how much he wanted this. How much he wanted *Abby*. He knew there would never be words enough to describe how much he wanted her...forever.

Abby pulled away from him and continued her work on releasing him from his jeans. Wyatt also desperately wanted to help her out of her clothes but the frantic way she was working on his clothing made it the best decision to stay out of her way for the moment. There would be time for him later. Losing a finger would not help the mood.

She was actually very quick about working the button and zipper. Wyatt made short work of kicking off his boots and sliding his underwear down to the ground. Somehow, he ended up completely naked and Abby was still wearing everything she'd shown up in.

That wasn't fair, not one bit.

Wyatt leaned into her, catching her lips with his. The kiss was flaming hot as they pressed furiously against each other. His hands worked feverishly to remove her soft blouse while maintaining their kiss.

Finally, he finished the last button. The fabric parted, revealing her lacy bra and her perfect breasts. Wyatt froze, taking in the sight. His fingers lightly brushed over the pale scars crisscrossing her stomach, and he knew from the extent of the damage that she'd been lucky to live through the accident.

He was lucky she lived through the accident. He didn't want to contemplate a life without Abby.

He finally ran his finger inside the waist of the well-fitted slacks, momentarily confused by the lack of snap or button on the front. Not wanting to show his lack of experience, he continued to slide his fingers around her waist, and found the hook and zipper right in the middle of her back.

There you are.

Wrapping his other arm around her, Wyatt pulled her close to him and used both hands to free her of the barrier between them, and he made it happen with only a little bit of fumbling. The smooth fabric slid silently down her legs and she stepped clear without removing her tongue from his mouth.

Wyatt finally broke the kiss by picking her up again. He carried her the last couple of steps to the bed and laid her down gently. He stood for just a moment, wanting to take her all in at once. Her perfect toes reached out towards him, sliding up and down his thighs as she let him look.

He felt himself stiffen further at the sight. She was so gorgeous. He'd been getting excited from the very beginning, of course, but this perfect woman lying there on his bed with *that* look in her eye…well, Wyatt couldn't help responding.

He reached down and hooked his fingers under the thin strings of fabric of her panties riding high over her hips and slipped the minuscule bit of lace off her body. He joined her on the bed, his knees landing between her opened thighs. His hands planted beside her head on the mattress. Bending his elbows, he kissed her, his need coming through his lips.

This kiss was just as hot as the one when they were standing, but this time, it was *more*. This was an invitation and he took it. Keeping their lips pressed tightly together, he lowered his hips and in one smooth motion, slid into her. Her heat, the moisture…she was going to be his undoing if he didn't hold himself back just a little. He had to last longer than this…

Her arms came up, wrapping around his back, her grip surprisingly strong and tight. She locked them together as he started rocking back and forth.

Wyatt desperately tried to express his love and desire for this woman with every thrust,

thinking the words *I love you* with every movement, a mantra building inside of him.

Finally, his control was gone and they
melded together and time froze. Nothing existed but them and their future that was just beginning. Wyatt's heart released a knot of
tension he didn't know he'd been holding onto,
and he allowed himself to become one with the
woman he loved.

EPILOGUE

ABBY

SHE LOOKED OUT into the bright sunshine outside the kitchen window. It was a gorgeous August day…as long as she stayed inside the house. It was too hot outside, even up in the mountains, but inside…she got to admire the sunshine without having to be baked in it.

She heard a hiss, a low woof, and then a yowl as Jasmine and Maggie Mae took off up the stairs. She could hear them tearing around the second story, a bump, and then a crash. With a half laugh, half cry, Abby dried her hands and headed up the stairs herself. If these two didn't kill each other soon, she might do it for them.

Ever since she'd moved into Wyatt's place – her childhood home – a month ago, they'd been doing their best to assassinate each other, often sneaking up on each other when one or the other was daring to actually take a nap. She figured they'd learn to like each other...right about the time the last lamp in the house was broken.

She went into the office and found Jasmine perched on top of her desk, hissing at Maggie, her back arched and her tail as big around as a Christmas ham. Maggie was pacing back and forth below her, trying to figure out how to get to the hissing cat without actually getting up on the furniture.

"Maggie Mae!" Abby bellowed and the dog instantly crouched, looking forlorn. "Go downstairs right now!" Maggie turned and trotted out of the room, her tail tucked between her legs.

"And you, young lady!" Abby turned to glare at her non-repentant cat who decided that since her arch enemy was gone from the room, it was petting time. Jasmine looked up at her, her big baby blues looking so mournful as she held a white paw up in the air.

"You have *got* to stop antagonizing Maggie Mae, pretty girl," Abby said, instantly softening towards her baby as Jasmine continued to look pitifully adorable. "We only have so much room in the lamp budget, you know."

She picked her up in her arms, cradling her against her chest, when she heard Wyatt's deep voice behind her. "Were they going at each other again?" he asked softly, leaning forward to nibble her neck.

"Ohhh," she said in a breathy voice, immediately forgetting all about the fights that had been tearing up the house. "What are you..." She sucked in her breath as he sucked her skin into his mouth.

And promptly forgot what she was about to ask him. She couldn't think at all when his mouth was doing that.

Or that...

He gently pulled away and turned her in

his arms, picking up Jasmine and setting her back down on the desk. He took her hand but instead of leading her to the bedroom, he led her down the stairs and out the front door.

"Where are we going?" she asked, confused. The lust had cleared away just enough for her to know that whatever he was doing, it wasn't normal. She'd expected him to be gone all day; they were getting into harvest season, and he should be out riding a tractor in straight rows, or planning their strategy with Jorge, or working with Declan and Stetson to get the tractors and trucks to the right place at the right time, or…

He pulled her up to the top of a small hill that overlooked a ravine stretching into the distance. This was one of her favorite places to go as a child, and even now, the view took her breath away. They stopped under an old mulberry tree, the red fruit beginning to ripen in the summer heat. They paused for a minute, just looking at the view, and then he turned to her, a look she couldn't read on his face. He took a deep breath.

"Abigail Gwen Connelly," he said, dropping to one knee in the cheat grass and dirt, "will you marry me?" He opened up a jewelry box to reveal a simple silver band in it – no stone, no glitter. He must've asked her father what jewelry could be worn while on duty.

It was...*perfect*.

"Oh Wyatt, yes!" she said, launching herself at him, and they rolled around in the cheat grass and dirt, laughing and kissing and she was getting poky shit in places she wouldn't want to mention but she didn't care because *yes*, she would marry Wyatt.

Suddenly, she stopped and pulled back and stared at him. "Are you sure?" she asked. "Really sure? You know I can't have kids and I don't...don't want you to resent me." Ever since that day that she'd been sent over to talk to him by her father, the topic of kids had lain between them, an unspoken topic of pain that she hadn't wanted to breach. He'd *said* that he was fine without them, but she saw how he was out at Adam's place. He was a natural with children. He deserved to be able to have them.

He deserved someone who wasn't broken like her.

"There you go, ruining the other half of my surprise," he said teasingly, giving her a peck on the cheek and scrambling to his feet and helping her up. "Here, look at these plans." He picked up a long roll of white paper that'd been leaning against the mulberry tree trunk. She couldn't believe she'd missed it; so much for her police training and paying attention to her surroundings. If it'd been a snake, it would've bit her.

He unrolled the plans and held them out for her to look at. She peered at them over his shoulder, trying to read them. It looked like a house. A really *big* house. "Do you want to build this house?" she asked, confused. It looked big enough to hold an army. Sure, their current house was a little on the cramped side, but they were making it work. They didn't need something that—

"Yes," he said, happiness lighting up his whole face as he turned and kissed her soundly on the cheek. "After you and I run off to Vegas and get hitched—"

"What?!" she yelped. "I don't want to get married in Vegas!"

"—then we can work on our certification to become foster parents," he finished, ignoring her protestations. She immediately forgot all about Vegas and just stared at him, mouth round with surprise.

"Foster parents?" she echoed.

"Working with the kids out at Adam's place…there's so many who need someone to love 'em," he said simply, shrugging. "But we need a bigger house if we're going to do it right."

"What are you going to do with the homestead?" she asked. Sure, the house they lived in was a little small, but it'd been in the Connelly family for generations. She didn't want to lose that history.

"Jorge. He and his family are stuffed into that double-wide. I figure that his kids or grandkids can move into the homestead. Or hell, him. I'm going to have the lawyer draw up the papers; Jorge can buy the house and the acre it's sitting on over the next five years. No interest. He deserves it, after keeping this place running while I wasn't here. For someone who hates to be dependent on others, that stint in jail taught me that without my family and Jorge, I would've been screwed."

He pulled her against him, stroking her hair as she nuzzled closer into his chest. It was hot as hell and she wouldn't be able to snuggle against him for much longer for fear of spontaneously combusting into flames, but for the moment, she wouldn't want to be anywhere else.

"Without you…I don't know where I'd be, or who I'd be. You are all I want or need, Abby. Although, once we get our certification to be foster parents, what do you think about Juan?"

Abby pulled back and stared up at his handsome face, the slight darkening from whiskers covering his jaw, his stormy blue eyes staring intently down at her. "You two really hit it off," she said softly. "I think he could really benefit from having someone like you in his life all the time, not just the occasional afternoons that you can make it out there."

She stroked her hand over his stubbled jaw and he turned to plant a kiss into the palm of it. "That's what I thought too. I haven't been able to go out there as much as I would've wanted since spring hit, but every time I do go out there…there's something about him, Abby. Make him a little taller and a little whiter, and he'd be me. A chip on his shoulder the size of Texas, but wanting to learn. Wanting to trust someone. I could make a difference with him, I know I could."

She felt tears spring to her eyes, and she leaned up and pecked him on the lips. "Darlin', I've never heard sexier words in all my life," she said softly.

"Sexy?" Wyatt said, laughing.

"Yeah. Damn sexy. In fact, I have an idea in mind." She took his hand and began tugging him back towards the house. He slipped the ring box back into his pocket, and she grinned to herself. He could slip it onto her finger later.

They had more important things to do just then.

Much more important.

∾

Quick Author's Note

OH, Wyatt.

I'm guessing that at this point, you've probably forgiven him for being an ass, but it was touch-and-go there for a while – am I right? Like Stetson, Wyatt can be…infuriating, to say the least. But finally seeing the world from his point of view, you get a bit more understanding of why he ended up the way he did.

After a really light and fluffy story like *Blizzard of Love*, *Arrested* is a lot more intense, with darker themes and more…meat on the bone, I guess. Writing it was my first chance to write a story with more depth and heart to it, but I found that I enjoyed it so much that virtually all books from here forward in my Long Valley world are more like *Arrested* and a lot less like

Blizzard. Not that there's more than one Wyatt out there (God forbid – I think the world might explode if there was more than one Wyatt occupying it) but rather that the storylines aren't always filled with sunshine and roses.

I do guarantee this, though: My *endings* will be filled with sunshine and roses. After all, isn't that why you read romance novels? I read one romance novel when I was a teenager where the guy died at the end of the book. I shit you not. I was *traumatized*.

Worst

Romance

Novel

Ever

Anyway, so after writing Wyatt's difficult past, I decided to tackle something even more difficult in my next book, *Returning for Love*. It's Declan's love story (of course! He's the last Miller brother. *Obviously* he needs to find love of his own) but in it, both Declan and Iris have ghosts from their pasts that they have to wrestle with. I'm not going to tell you what they are because finding out is part of the story and I'm not gonna ruin it for you, but I promise you, you're gonna be snuffling happily by the end of it. I hope you choose to pick it up from your favorite library or bookstore – it's available wherever you get your reading fix!

Hugs,
Erin Wright

ALSO BY ERIN WRIGHT

~ LONG VALLEY ~

Accounting for Love

Blizzard of Love

Arrested by Love

Returning for Love

Christmas of Love

Overdue for Love

Bundle of Love

Lessons in Love

Baked with Love

Bloom of Love (2021)

Holly and Love (TBA)

Banking on Love (TBA)

Sheltered by Love (TBA)

Conflicted by Love (TBA)

~ FIREFIGHTERS OF LONG VALLEY ~

Flames of Love

Inferno of Love

Fire and Love

Burned by Love

~ MUSICIANS OF LONG VALLEY ~

Strummin' Up Love

Melody of Love (TBA)

Rock 'N Love (TBA)

Rhapsody of Love (TBA)

~ SERVICEMEN OF LONG VALLEY ~

Thankful for Love (2021)

Commanded to Love (TBA)

Salute to Love (TBA)

Harbored by Love (TBA)

ABOUT ERIN WRIGHT

USA Today Bestselling author Erin Wright has worked every job under the sun, including library director, barista, teacher, website designer, and ranch hand helping brand cattle, before settling into the career she's always dreamed about: Author.

She still loves coffee, doesn't love the smell of cow flesh burning, and has embarked on the adventure of a lifetime, traveling the country full-time in an RV. (No one has died yet in the confined 250-square-foot space – which she considers a real win – but let's be real, next week isn't looking so good…)

Find her updates on ErinWright.net, where you can sign up for her newsletter along with the requisite pictures of Jasmine the Writing

Cat, her kitty cat muse and snuggle buddy extraordinaire.

Wanna get in touch?
www.erinwright.net
erin@erinwright.net

Or reach out to Erin on your favorite social media platform:

f facebook.com/AuthorErinWright

twitter.com/erinwrightlv

pinterest.com/erinwrightbooks

goodreads.com/erinwright

BB bookbub.com/profile/erin-wright

instagram.com/authorerinwright

Printed in the USA
CPSIA information can be obtained
at www.ICGtesting.com
LVHW022143241023
762064LV00011B/242